T0149609

SILENCE
—IS THE—
WAYFARER OF
JUDGMENT

Jordan Bennett

authorHOUSE®

AuthorHouse™
1663 Liberty Drive
Bloomington, IN 47403
www.authorhouse.com
Phone: 1 (800) 839-8640

Published by AuthorHouse 09/21/2016

ISBN: 978-1-5246-3890-0 (sc)
ISBN: 978-1-5246-3888-7 (hc)
ISBN: 978-1-5246-3889-4 (e)

Library of Congress Control Number: 2016914836

Print information available on the last page.

This book is dedicated to my sister, Jennifer,
for everything.
Special thanks to Scott Hensley at Author House
and attorney Andrew Stout
for their help in bringing this book to print.

Memories of Death

I recently traveled back to the small town in which I grew up. Through life I've noticed many such small towns, but growing up, I was sure there was no other place like Maple Falls. It was the only world I knew. But I was innocent then and noticed only what my developing mind wanted to see: a superficial world that was created by, and catered to, my dreams and wishes.

Like all kids, I had a physical and emotional attachment to my home town. It happens to almost all of us: one day we are living a dream created by ourselves, and then something happens, and suddenly we get a glimpse of the real world. From that point on, we've lost the innocence of childhood and belong to the adult world. I guess that is the difference between a child's world and an adult's world. A child's world caters and conforms to the child's needs and wishes, whereas the adult world does not. The world is rigid and uncompromising; the adult is the one who has to give and take to fit in.

I had not given much thought to my early childhood for quite some time and had almost forgotten the past. But to be honest, the memories of Maple Falls— especially the month that brought me from childhood to adulthood—have always occupied a place at the back of my mind. I can never forget that experience.

Now I find myself thinking of that month quite often as I recall a trip home. I had traveled with my wife and two daughters back to Maple Falls to attend a funeral, and the memories came with the trip. Though the incident from my childhood seemed to last for years, it really only spanned a few months.

I was eleven the summer I lost my innocence. Kids have experienced many traumatic, life-changing events: poverty, violence, or some other occurrence. For me, it was a death. I had been to a few funerals before that summer, so I had already seen a dead person, but no death affected me like the death I faced then. And the truth is I never saw a dead body that summer—only heard about it—but I was still greatly affected. Death will do that to you sometimes.

I was eleven that summer and living in a world all my own. Fewer than five hundred people lived in Maple Falls, and though it was rare for any major events to take place (events I only realized existed when I moved away from Maple Falls), there was still plenty to keep a young child busy. I never heard of any murders or robberies or other crimes taking place while I lived there. I'm sure there was crime in Maple Falls, but it wasn't prevalent, like in most of the larger cities. Being a child, I didn't hear about the little bit of crime that did occur. Tucker's barn burned down one summer, and that brought every kid from town to watch—every kid except the Barlow twins. The only time the two of them were seen was at school or Sunday church. I wonder what happened to the Barlow twins. I wonder why they never had any friends. I asked a few people at the funeral if they knew what happened to the Barlow family, but no one seemed to know. They just up and moved one year, and no one I asked ever heard of them again.

The main event each year was the small parade held every Labor Day and the traveling carnival that came for a week to help celebrate the event. The rest of the time, a kid was left to his own imagination and initiative.

I lived with my family on the outskirts of town, and since there was only one other house within a quarter mile, I became good friends with one of the boys who lived there. At the time, I thought he was my best friend. We did just about everything together, from riding our bikes into town to watch a matinee or hang around the soda shop to following the town creek out to our favorite fishing and swimming hole. But best friends don't keep secrets from each other. At least that's how I felt then. Until that summer though, life was the best for us.

Larry came from a large family of three sisters and two brothers. Though Larry was my best friend, I didn't know the rest of his family that well. His father worked in Windy Corners, which was fifteen miles south of Maple Falls. He would say hi to me when he was home, but he always seemed to be busy fixing one thing or another and didn't have time to be bothered with us kids. Larry's brothers and sisters had their own friends from school, so they were often with them. (It never occurred to me that his brothers and sisters usually went over their friends' houses to play, just as Larry and I rarely played at his house.) I almost never saw his mother. I had often heard my mother tell others that Mrs. Thompson was a homebody and only occasionally left her house. With Larry and me playing in town or along the river most the time, I didn't even notice when she stopped going outside altogether.

As I look back now, I realize there were many things I didn't notice at the beginning of that summer. I suppose part of it may have been that I was innocent then and naive as to what was really happening around me. Larry and I still played together, as in years past, but his attitude had changed. He seemed to be more serious, more preoccupied. He didn't laugh or joke around as much. If I thought anything, it was probably that it was what happened when someone reached his age.

He was two years older, so I just expected him to lead the way into the different stages of life. I don't know how I could have thought anything different.

Even though Larry and his siblings played at their friends' houses quite often, I would still say they were a close family. They did a lot of things together; they just didn't do much together as a family with outsiders. But that summer, all the kids in Larry's family started to spend even more time with their friends away from their home. I didn't know they were trying to escape from something. It is easy now to make a connection between everything that happened that summer and the death we faced. But that's because I know more about life now; it's always easier to make connections between events after the fact.

I began to learn the truth one evening when I returned from town. I had gone by myself that day. Larry said he had some work to do around his house, so being by myself I was home earlier than usual. My mother had a few of her lady friends over; they were talking when I entered through the kitchen door, so I'm sure they didn't notice that I was home. I was about to head for the washroom to clean up when my mother mentioned something about Mrs. Thompson. I stopped to listen. I always listened when anything was said about Larry's mother, as there was an air of mystery about her. But I was unprepared for what they said.

"I heard they brought her home early this morning in an ambulance."

"She was taken into her house on a stretcher. I think she's confined to her bed now."

I'm not sure who was talking; I was only able to distinguish my mother's voice when she spoke. But it only mattered what was said.

"I didn't even know she was sick."

"Neither did I. And to think, I'm her neighbor. The family has always kept pretty much to themselves. I mean, the children do have their friends, but I noticed they never talked about their family life that much."

"What you say is true. I heard earlier this morning that she has been sick for quite some time."

"Why did they bring her home if she's so sick?"

"I heard that Lois believes it's not God's way to use man-made medicines for cures."

I've come to realize over the years that *heard* is a very powerful word. In the days that followed, I *heard* many things. I heard that Mrs. Thompson was sick with cancer and had been sick for quite some time. But *sick* was not the right word to use; she was dying. I didn't see Larry at all during those first few days, so I had plenty of time to think about what I heard. I found it almost impossible to believe that Mrs. Thompson could be sick and dying. Surely Larry would have said something to me.

I had a clear view of Larry's house from my upstairs bedroom window, so I watched his house during the morning hours those first few days after Mrs. Thompson returned home. I'm not sure what I was hoping to see. Maybe what I really needed was some kind of proof that what I had heard was true or that it wasn't true. I needed to know either way. But I never caught a glimpse of an ambulance coming to the house or cars coming and going in succession to see the sick. In fact, there was nothing out of the ordinary to see. It appeared that life was going on normally at the Thompson house. It's true that I never saw Larry's mother go outside those few days. I did see his father a couple of times, but then, if I thought about it, I hadn't noticed Mrs. Thompson outside for quite a while.

On the fourth morning after I first heard the news about Mrs. Thompson, I was called from my room and told that Larry was waiting to see me. I had just awakened, so my morning vigil by the window had not yet begun. Otherwise I would have been aware of his arrival. In the minute or so it took me to walk from my room to the front door, I decided I was going to wait for Larry to be the first to say something about his mother. I was sure that was what he wanted to see me about— to explain to me the truth of what I'd heard. Besides, I didn't think I could bring myself to be the first to mention his mother's illness.

There seemed to be a hesitation in the air as we walked away from my house that day; as I think back, I realize it was inside me. Larry was the same as he had been all summer. He was different from previous summers, but he had not changed during the past few months. And if I hadn't noticed the change in him earlier in the summer, I shouldn't have noticed it then. So the hesitation and nervousness rested with me, though at the time I thought it rested with him.

We made our way uptown, and soon we were talking about all our usual topics: baseball, which movie was showing at the matinee, and what we'd heard about the other kids in town. We spent the day as we usually did, and by evening it almost seemed like old times. A part of me kept wondering if what I had heard about Larry's mother was true. Maybe a joke was being played on everyone; how else could Larry act as if nothing was wrong?

When I got home that night, my mother was quick to ask if Larry had mentioned his mother's condition. When I told her Larry hadn't said anything, she made a comment about how some people keep pain and suffering bottled up inside. That was their way to deal with grief and pain.

That night I decided I was going to find out the truth for myself. At the time, I wasn't sure how, but I just knew I had to. Larry and I continued to play together; he stopped by to see me almost every other day. I was hoping he would eventually tell me about his mother, but he was determined to remain silent. By the end of the week, I realized I had only two options to discover the truth: I could ask Larry about his mother, or I could go and see her myself. Since I had decided I could never bring up the subject to Larry, I only had one choice.

As I think back now, I am surprised how rationally my mind worked under those conditions, considering I was only eleven at the time. Or maybe it's that the mind of an eleven-year-old can only work on the simplest level, for the plan I devised was really the simplest option. I could have gone over to Larry's house and asked to see him, but if his mother was really dying, the family probably wouldn't let me in the house. And there was no other pretense I could use to get into the house that made any sense to me. (I'm sure my mind wasn't working logically, but again, the uncomplicated mind of a child could see the only thing to do would be to sneak over to Larry's house and somehow get a glimpse of his mother.)

I suppose I had in me at the time the closest thing to an obsession an eleven-year-old boy could have. It slowly grew in me until I just had to see Mrs. Thompson. And it was no longer about discovering the truth but seeing her dying. Somewhere along the way, my mind had decided Mrs. Thompson was dying, and now I just wanted to see what someone looked like who was more dead than alive. To me, nothing else mattered.

Within a few days, the opportunity presented itself where I could sneak out of the house without worrying about being caught. My parents were attending a dance in Windy Corners and had hired Mrs. Cathers to sit for me. Now, Mrs. Cathers was a strict woman (I only got on her bad side one time, and that was cause enough for me to never provoke her anger again). But once she was seated in our old rocker and working on her knitting with the radio playing gospel music in the background, she could be counted on not to move until my parents came home—barring an earth-shattering emergency. I knew this to be a fact because Larry and I had snuck out and caused mischief in town more than once while Mrs. Cathers was sitting for me.

Fear is a very powerful emotion in a child, and I was full of fear as I climbed out my window and down the trellis on that moonless night. It was not the fear of being caught or the fear of the night and its darkness that confronted me. No, it was the fear of the unknown I faced that night—the fear of death. Death was heavy in the air, and I felt its every pulse. I believe the fear I experienced (a fear whose likeness I have not tasted since) would have turned back many a child, but it just shows how much of an obsession was in me to allow me to continue on in spite of that fear.

I knew the trail to Larry's house well; we had worn the grass away years before and had used the trail almost daily since. But that night, I had trouble finding my way in the dark; fear can block so much out of one's mind. After what seemed like an eternity—but was in fact just a few hundred beats of my heart—I was at the corner of the Thompson house. I knew where Mrs. Thompson's bedroom was, but when I stopped at the corner of the house, I became momentarily confused. I believe I partly wanted to listen to the fear and turn around, but the thought of seeing death spurred me on. Soon I was underneath Mrs. Thompson's window.

A blind made of wooden slats covered the window, but the light slipped through the cracks. I never considered the possibility that the light in her room would be turned off. I guess I figured if she was sick, there would be a light on—even if just a dim one—and someone would be attending her. I looked along the cracks until I found two slats far enough apart which allowed me to see into the room, which allowed me to see everything.

Mrs. Thompson was definitely dying, of that there could be no doubt. She was propped up in her bed by pillows, and there was an array of liquid-filled glasses on the nightstand beside the bed. Though the room was not brightly lit, I could still see enough. I was aware there were chairs situated around her bed in which her children sat. Mr. Thompson stood at the head of the bed beside his wife. They were all there, from David, the oldest, to Katy, the youngest, but I was still able to see around them to Mrs. Thompson. I was conscious of these facts, although my eyes never left Mrs. Thompson's face. It was evident that she was in pain and had been for some time. It was etched across her forehead and pulled at the corners of her eyes and mouth. Her skin was not white, which I thought it would be, but rather a mottled gray which speckled her exposed skin. Her skin was wrapped tightly around her bones—more like bandages than a layer of skin—and she lay quite still. I thought she might already be dead, but then her head moved slowly to the side, as if to acknowledge someone talking.

I wondered how her children could sit around her while she was in that condition. They sat like spectators, and I suppose in a sense they were. They couldn't have enjoyed sitting there watching their mother dying; why else would they have stayed away from their house during the day? I could only see two of the children's faces, and on them I could see not only a look of complete devotion but also something akin to being hypnotized by what they saw. And the unbelievable thing was I found myself drawn into their world. I was transfixed by the figure that lay on the bed and could not turn away.

Mrs. Thompson looked from one child to another; as she looked at each of them, they said something to her. When this was done, Mrs. Thompson seemed to relax a little. Her head sank back into the pillows, and her eyes fixed themselves to the space in front of her, and straight at the window where I was watching. She remained still for a moment, and then her eyes widened. This time I would say her skin tone did turn a ghostly white. When she tried to raise her hand, I was sure she was going to point at the window, and at me. At that moment the spell the figure held over me was broken. I moved back from the house, and, without any thought of returning to the window, I turned and ran home.

I was certain at the time that Mrs. Thompson had seen me outside her window or at least a glimpse of my shape. It is something I will never be sure of, for I never saw Mrs. Thompson again because she died later that same night. And just as Larry never said anything about his mother's illness, he also never mentioned her death. In fact, very little was ever said about her death. There was no obituary in the newspaper and no announcement of a funeral. I heard later that, early one morning a few days after the death, the immediate family gathered at the small cemetery on the outskirts of town and buried her. I cannot even recall hearing about anyone outside the family witnessing the event. Mrs. Thompson suffered and died as ambiguously as she had lived.

Over the years, I have heard how people, before they die, sometimes say they see something that isn't there. Whether it is an aspect of their lives they're reliving or the specter of death itself coming to claim them, I cannot say. So as I have grown older, I have tried to tell myself that there was something else Mrs. Thompson saw the night she died, that it wasn't me she caught a glimpse of. But a part of me cannot believe that and probably never will. Even if she only caught a glimpse of my shadow and was frightened by it, I hate to think I was the cause of her dying that night. But again, I will never know.

Larry and I continued to play together but not as often as before. And though he never said anything to me about his mother, he appeared to be a changed person. He suddenly seemed much older; he wasn't as interested in the games we had played since childhood. But then again, neither was I. We began to see less and less of each other, even as the summer turned into fall. I'm sure there would have come a day when we would have stopped seeing each other altogether. But then my family moved away from Maple Falls. My father's brother had obtained a better job for him in another state.

I never saw or heard from Larry again after my family moved out of Maple Falls. For many years I blamed Larry for the end of our friendship. If he had really been my best friend, he would have told me about his mother. But recalling that summer now, I realize that maybe Larry dealt with it the only way he knew how. He had had to watch his mother pass away before his eyes, while she would not accept any help in her illness. I know now that even best friends must deal with some grief in a solitary way.

So we were the best of friends back then whose friendship only existed in the innocence of childhood. As we grew older, we realized we didn't need each other any longer. And Larry and I both aged a lot the summer I was eleven—the summer we learned about death. That summer Larry and I lost our friendship. Death will do that to you sometimes.

The Last Bullet

There are some things a person should never have to do or even consider. And yet here I am, in the darkest hours of the night, caressing my daughter's cheek and forehead as she sleeps, while I wonder when it is I'm going to kill her. It doesn't make me feel any better to tell myself I'm really saving her, it's the best thing I can do for her under the circumstances, and it has to be done. When it really comes down to it, I'm killing my child, and that's something a parent should never do.

In the faint glow created by the dwindling embers in the fireplace I can see movement underneath Aileen's eyelids as she dreams. She'll wake up soon, but when she sees me sitting by her, watching over her, she'll quickly fall back to sleep. It's been like this the whole week we've been here at the cabin. If she knew what was on my mind, would she still be comforted by my presence or would she think of me as a monster? How could an eight-year-old child understand what I have to do? And how can I consider killing someone who means the world to me?

From the moment Aileen was born, my life changed dramatically. I had been excited when my wife, Brooke, announced she was pregnant. As the months passed by, I thought I would be ready when the day came for our baby to be born, but I was completely blown away when I got my first look at the life I helped bring into the world. I was in the room with my wife during the delivery and stayed by her side during the procedure. We had decided we would be together when we saw our child for the first time. When I finally set eyes on my daughter, I was surprised to find out how emotionally unprepared I was.

I thought I had known what complete love was when I married Brooke, but I was wrong. I loved my wife and still ached when I thought about her. But the way I can describe my love for her was that it was based on certain guidelines, certain conditions. We were two separate people who were connected only by our desires to be with each other and an attraction that drew us together. That kind of love is a fragile bond that can be broken; thankfully, Brooke and I never faced that dilemma.

The love of a child is something completely different. It is not based on wanting to develop a relationship on multifaceted levels. With a son or daughter the love is there from the start. It is unconditional love. That child is a part of you, so there is no thought of that individual being separate from you. And to know you had a part in the creation of that life holds the child to you in a unique bond.

Even though I felt a strong fatherly connection to Aileen before Brooke's death, that unfortunate event really cemented the bond between us. In some ways it was a blessing that Aileen was so young when her mother died. For even though I could see the confusion in her eyes and the questions she had about her mother's absence, she was young enough to eventually forget her mother's physical aspects. I know that sounds callous, but I'm sure it saved Aileen years of deep pain that I experienced.

In many ways Aileen was a saving grace for me when Brooke died. I was devastated by the loss; I may not have made it through the ordeal on my own. I still have days when I feel like throwing it all in, but I have to continue on because of Aileen and my responsibility to her. Any day

I feel depressed, a voice in my mind reminds me of that responsibility. It helps to remember how my daughter looks at me with unconditional love and need.

I've heard it said that good eventually comes out of something bad, and that was especially true of Brooke's death. I had quite a wild side to me before I married Brooke. Although married life had calmed me down a little I still found time to go to bars and parties. The birth of Aileen cut even more into my wild lifestyle, but knowing Brooke was at home with our daughter gave me the excuse to meet up with my buddies once or twice a week. After Brooke died, all the responsibility for Aileen fell fully on my shoulders. Even after I got over the worst of my depression, I still did not want to leave Aileen if I didn't have to. I needed her as much as she needed me.

As time went by, so many things that might appear minor to others were just magnified by my love for my daughter. They included the way her small hand reached for mine and nestled so comfortably within it and the way her blue, doe-shaped eyes would look at me when I picked her up from daycare and then school. There was no doubt I was the world to her, and that made her so much more the world to me. That is why the situation we now find ourselves in is even more terrifying.

The plague that brought us to this point started a little over two weeks ago. At first it was touted as just a new and more virulent strain of flu. At that point, most people didn't give it a second thought. We've become so accustomed to new flu strains that even when the deaths started, it didn't faze us that much; there were flu-related deaths every year. The only concern I really had was wondering if Aileen had received her flu shot for the current year. Outbreaks continued popping up everywhere, and when Aileen's school closed at the end of that first week because of large absenteeism, I decided to take her to the cabin. I still wasn't too concerned at that point; I just wanted to get Aileen and myself away from people who might be sick.

Aileen was excited when I told her where we were going. We had not visited the cabin often after her mother died. Aileen was only two when Brooke died and didn't remember much about her mother, but the cabin held for me so many memories of Brooke that it had been painful the few times Aileen and I visited there. Over the years, I had even considered selling the cabin, but now I was thankful I hadn't.

For the past six years, my main concern has been to nurture and care for my little girl. Because I was raising Aileen on my own, I felt an overpowering sense of responsibility and an unbreakable—sometimes almost unbearable—love for her. I understand what people mean when they say they would do anything for someone. For Aileen I would have gone to the ends of the earth. I know that's an overused cliché, but it's true.

There was a small, battery-operated radio in the cabin. Because I was used to the television on or music playing during the day at home, I turned the radio on soon after we settled into the cabin for background noise rather than for information. Music played on most stations, with updates of the virus being transmitted every few hours or so. By the end of our second day at the cabin, there were more news reports about the virus worldwide than there was music playing. Soon there were only news reports. Vaccinations weren't working, hospitals were full, and people were dying at a frightening rate. Martial law had been declared, and it seemed that society was completely breaking down.

Even though I felt a small sense of security by being secluded in the woods, I knew with society collapsing anything was possible, so I had to remain vigilant. The cabin was quite rustic; it had a hand pump in the kitchen and a generator in a small shed out back. To save fuel we would use lanterns after dark, and I would build a fire in the fireplace only if it got chilly. Luckily I had brought some food and water with us; some canned goods were still stocked in the cabin, Aileen and I could hold out until it was clear what the end result of the virus would be.

What put me on edge the most was that there was only one bullet for the handgun I had stored at the cabin. I had thought there was a full box of ammo with the handgun, but I couldn't find it. When Aileen was born, Brooke didn't want a gun in the house, so I stored the gun at the cabin. When I decided to take Aileen to the cabin after the outbreak, I remembered the gun but didn't think much else about it. When I heard what was happening around the world, I thought I could use the gun for some kind of protection if need be. And then I found only the one bullet.

When the radio reports became dire, I decided to listen only after Aileen went to sleep or when I knew her attention was diverted elsewhere. I didn't want her to know how bad things had gotten. To occupy Aileen during the day we played some card games. I also found some old photo albums with pictures of her mother, and we looked through them while I told her stories of when the photos had been taken. The whole time only one thought preyed on my mind: how could I protect my little girl if someone with bad intentions found us?

That had been my main concern until this past afternoon. Aileen and I had been looking through another photo album when she coughed. It wasn't the body-shaking, hard cough the news reports had talked about, but, to me, it was a staggering blow. Aileen was so interested in the photographs I don't think she even realized she had coughed. At least she didn't act as though she realized what the possible implications might be. I'm sure she didn't notice how my body stiffened when I heard it.

The rest of the afternoon I felt sick to my stomach, thinking Aileen might have the virus. I felt helpless. The medical community was in shambles, so it would be useless to try to take her to a doctor or a hospital. There was some over-the-counter cold and flu medicine at the cabin, but it would be useless if Aileen had the virus. A child expects a parent to take care of him or her, but if she did have the virus, I'd be completely unable to help her. I don't even want to think what might happen if the fever set in and she became delirious. Some reports stated that when delirium set in, victims would become quite violent before a coma and then death occurred. The media relayed stories of the sick injuring or even killing family members or friends while delirious.

Aileen coughed a few more times during the afternoon, and each time it was like a dagger pushing deeper into my chest. I was fortunate each time that she didn't see the pain and worry in my eyes. By keeping her away from the radio and immersed in the card games or the photo albums she didn't fully realize what the implications of her cough meant. But I knew if Aileen kept coughing or it got worse, she would eventually realize she had caught the flu. Could I sound convincing if I tried to tell her it was just a cold and that it would be all right?

Everything changed after Aileen fell asleep, and a cough escaped from me. And it wasn't one of those small, tickle-in-the-throat coughs. Suddenly my whole thought process changed. I tried to convince myself—or at least give myself hope in the possibility—that maybe all Aileen had was a common, everyday cold. My cough was already so much worse than hers. I felt certain I was suffering from the virus even if she just had a plain cold.

My thoughts of that last bullet had also changed dramatically. First it had been a resource of defense. Then when Aileen started to cough, I looked at that last bullet as an escape for me. If Aileen was sick with the virus and died, what reason would I have to go on? My purpose for living—my little girl—would be gone. With the rest of the world falling to pieces it would just be easier to use the bullet on myself.

Those plans changed again when I started to cough. With Aileen asleep I had a lot of time to think about what our coughs might mean. I had no desire to sleep anyway, so all there was to do was work out a possible solution to the problem I now faced. I can't describe my exact thought process, but after watching Aileen sleep for a while, I suddenly knew what I had to do—not that the solution comforted me. It seemed so logical but also so cold and impersonal. Maybe it was my way of dealing with the guilt my solution posed, but making it impersonal didn't change the facts. The bullet now was not for me but for Aileen.

So here is the reasoning behind my thoughts. If Aileen was sick with the virus, I had a way to keep her from suffering. The reports on the radio stated the sickness was quite an ordeal to go through before dying. With the bullet, it would be quick. The thought of smothering her with a pillow worried me; she might wake up, and I wouldn't want that. I also didn't know if I could go through with it if she started to struggle. And even if Aileen wasn't sick with the virus, it didn't change matters much because there was a good chance I had the virus. With the coughs, fever, and body aches I was experiencing, I was fairly sure of it. And if I became delirious before I took action, there was also a good chance I could harm or kill Aileen before lapsing into a coma. Even if I didn't harm Aileen, I couldn't leave her alone in this cursed and damned world.

So my plan was this. While Aileen was asleep—and may God forgive me for this—I would use the bullet on her. If I was still coherent in the morning and had the energy, I would bury her behind the cabin. I would clean her up, put her in the best clothes she had brought, and then bury her. After that, nothing else would matter. Maybe I would head back to the city to meet my fate. The sooner it was all over with the better.

After reviewing this plan, I decided to wait a little while longer before taking action. Listening to her breathe comforted me. It reminded me of the joy she had brought to my life. Her eyelids were fluttering as she dreamed. She was whimpering a little; her dreams must be troubled. I thought to myself, *She'll wake up soon, and I'll comfort her like a parent should and help her fall back to sleep. I can wait for that. Soon I'll make sure her troubled dreams are gone forever. I'll save her from the curse we now face.*

I hate the world for bringing us to this point and myself for what I have to do now. But it's the best thing I can do for my little girl.

Voices from a Distant Past

I watched as Sylvia moved slowly into the room. It had been a long time since I stayed awake waiting for her to come home. There was a time when I lay awake many nights waiting for her, but that had been when things were different between us. Now all that was left were the memories of what had been.

If I had not watched Sylvia so many times in the past, I would have thought I was dreaming; she moved so gracefully. That was one of the qualities I had found alluring in her from the start, and it was one of the few qualities that still drew me to her. Even now, when all the closeness and love have left our marriage, I still find myself attracted to and excited by the figure that moved so gracefully through the dimly-lit room. As Sylvia began to undress at the foot of the bed, I wondered who she had been with—not that it mattered any longer. She undressed to her panties before slipping under the covers beside me. I remained still for a moment and then rolled closer toward her.

When our relationship first started, we had slept together differently; Sylvia usually fell asleep with her head on my chest. But as the years went by, she moved further away from me until, like now, she lay on her side with her back to me. Over time I had learned how to shape my body to the curve of hers, and for the past several years, I slept huddled up to her back with my arm around her, hugging her to me. I huddled up to her again. But, as had been the case for so long, I could feel no warmth from her. It also felt like a coldness was emanating from her. I forced myself to remain beside her. Tonight I needed to feel that cold.

"Good-night, baby," Sylvia said as she took my hand and rested it on her breast. I find it amazing that she shows me any affection at all, since our relationship long ago ceased to be based on love. We didn't need each other; there were even times when we said we no longer wanted each other, but we always stayed together. We fought often over the years; though we separated several times, we always returned to each other. We both knew from the start we had our differences. We tried to bridge them, but we were never able to do so completely.

My mind wandered as I softly began to kiss Sylvia on the nape of her neck. I thought back to the beginning; it was easier that way. I cannot say why Sylvia stayed with me through the years, but for me it had more to do with resignation than anything else. From the beginning, I had been aware that our relationship had the potential to crumble to its current condition. But back then, I tried to overlook that fact because I loved her. I had only recently ended a long relationship, and I was determined to try harder to make the one with Sylvia work. Though I wished for a deeper relationship with her, it was better than having no relationship at all—at least I felt that way then. I needed someone, and she was there. In reality I just didn't want to be alone.

From the start I knew what she was like, but she had done a good job of keeping her private life separate from the relationship we began to build. She became the friend I needed. She listened to my pains and dreams and gave me the support and affection I needed. For all those reasons I fell in love with her. And I believe, at one time, Sylvia loved me (at least I hope so) because if she didn't, it meant that she had played me from the beginning. She seemed excited by my dreams and said that she would like to be a part of them. She helped me through my problems and made me feel important, and needed.

It was inevitable that Sylvia's private life would eventually surface in our relationship. She went on one of her binges, and I saw for the first time the ugly side of the woman I loved. I had nothing against going to parties to see friends and have a good time; I often did it myself. And entertaining clients was a part of both our professions. But Sylvia almost lived for those parties. She would disregard our relationship as long as she was able to attend her parties. If I planned anything for us to do together and a party was announced, my plans were forgotten. And it didn't matter whether I went to the party with her or not because she was going.

As the years passed, I realized we would never make each other happy. I'm not saying the relationship was bad all the time because it wasn't. We had many good times together, but it seemed with each passing year we both became a little colder, a little more callous toward each other. The thought of divorce had entered my mind many times, but I could never bring myself to discuss it with Sylvia or even seriously consider it myself. I felt divorce would not only be killing our marriage, but it would destroy part of me. When I married Sylvia, I devoted to her a portion of myself I had never given to anyone else, and I was afraid that if we divorced, I would never get it back. I was growing to hate what she had become, but I still loved her for the woman I had once known.

Sylvia also gave me hope that things would change. After her parties, she would say how sorry she was to disappoint me and how she wanted to change for us. She said it was the lifestyle she had grown up with, and she needed time to change. If only we could get away and start our lives anew, things would be different. But we never got away; we were never able to start our lives over. Finally I resigned myself to the fact that things would never change.

Sylvia moaned softly as I caressed her body. I knew what was going to happen next. We would make love without love again tonight. Though most of the love had left our relationship, we never stopped having sex. Even when we both found other people to share our affections with we still eventually came home to each other. The sex satisfied my, and I'm sure Sylvia's, carnal desires. That was another reason the thought of divorce frightened me; I didn't want someone else to completely have her. We might not have much, but at least we still gave some of ourselves to each other.

As I moved my hand from her breast down across her flat stomach, Sylvia opened her legs. I continued to caress her, bringing her desires closer to the surface. I removed her panties, and she hitched a leg back over my hip. She was ready and so was I, the act was soon to be complete. She didn't say anything as she guided me into her. As I entered her, I thought back to all the broken promises she had given me—that we had given each other—and all the spoken dreams we had never fulfilled, and it saddened me. Even with all the issues we had in our relationship we had been happy at one time, but somewhere along the way we lost that happiness. Just as sex can be a selfish act to gratify one's needs, we had grown selfish in our relationship, thinking only of ourselves. Now it no longer mattered.

As I neared orgasm, I knew things would soon be different, and in that knowledge I found comfort. I reached under the pillow and closed my hand to the cold. With our bodies moving in unison, I brought my hand from under the pillow to her back, to the base of her neck. As we both began to shake with orgasm—ironically, the first time we had ever climaxed simultaneously during intercourse—I pulled my finger.

The force of the bullet ripping through her throat tore her from me and threw her across the bed. I lay still for a moment as I waited for my body to stop shaking, and then, after throwing the revolver across the room and onto the floor, I reached out to Sylvia. A warmth flowed from her body; it had been such a long time since I had felt warmth from her, and I huddled closer to her. Letting the warmth flow over me, I heard in my mind, for the last time, the promises we had shared with each other so long ago. And as the voices faded, I leaned over Sylvia and kissed her on the cheek, crying softly as I whispered her name.

The Water Lilies

We all go through life maturing from the experiences we face. As they mold our characters, we become a product of them. A first love, a death in the family, a broken heart, views and opinions from friends and family, and guilt: we mature through all these things. Of these, guilt can have a strong impact on the direction our lives take. Guilt can grow in us like a cancer until it is all consuming. All we can hope for is to be forgiven for our indiscretions. And often, forgiveness has to come from within ourselves. Others involved can forgive us for the guilt we feel; but if we can't forgive ourselves, we'll never really begin to heal. That's not to say forgiveness from others isn't beneficial or even necessary. But sometimes the person we need forgiveness from cannot give it, and that also can have an impact on our personal healing.

There are two reasons why my younger sister, Lizzie, could not give me the forgiveness I so desperately needed. The first and most obvious reason was that she died ten years ago at the age of thirteen. But even if she hadn't died, I could not have received the forgiveness I sought from her. This second reason that would have prevented her forgiving me was the fact that she suffered from schizophrenia catatonia. She never spoke and had to be fed, clothed, and bathed. She was incapable of existing by herself in our world.

So often an older sibling will guide and protect a younger one, and I wish now I had been that person for Lizzie when we were children; unfortunately, I wasn't. I fell into a different group of kids—the ones who make fun of those with disadvantages. I don't want to believe or to admit that I was mean-spirited as a child, but I still made fun of my sister along with my friends. She was a dunce, a dimwit, a vegetable. I even think I was the first one in my circle of friends to call her what became our main description for her: "freak." I realize now I didn't treat Lizzie badly out of hatred; I was just embarrassed by her.

Despite this situation, my early years were not much different from those of other kids. My family, which consisted of my parents, my older brother, Will, Lizzie, and I, lived in a modest house in upstate New York. There was a small lake behind the house, and Mother used to like to sit by it and paint the lake, using as focal points the ducks and geese that landed in numbers on its surface or the water lilies that covered its edges. In my opinion, Mother was an atrocious painter, but as it kept her occupied and she usually took Lizzie along with her, her hobby left me free to play with my friends. So I never told her how I felt.

More than giving me the opportunity to play with my friends, I was grateful Mother took Lizzie down to the lake with her when she painted because then I didn't have to look after my sister. Still there were times when I had to take care of her, and I resented Mother for that. Luckily, Will had to do that chore more often than I did. He was the older sibling who looked out after the weak one. Will never complained or said bad things about Lizzie. I'm sure he knew how I referred to her, but aside from a few disgusted looks he gave me when the subject of Lizzie came up and I hinted at my feelings he never said anything to me about it.

So Mother would take Lizzie down to the lake with her when she painted. Mother had not always painted, and as I think of that period of my life, I believe she began to do so after Lizzie learned to walk. That in itself represented a miracle to Mother and Father. Lizzie still had to be led, otherwise she might aimlessly wander off, but at least she could walk.

The trips Mother and Lizzie made to the lake went on uneventfully for a few years until one summer day when Lizzie was eight. I was playing with some friends on that momentous day, so I didn't hear the story until dinner time, when Mother could not stop talking about it. It seemed that while Mother and my sister were by the lake, Lizzie had picked up a brush and started painting on a canvas as Mother was getting herself a cup of tea. We all looked at Lizzie, but she sat like she always did, staring blankly in front of her.

I couldn't understand how Mother, Father, and Will could get so excited about Lizzie doodling with a paint brush, but then I guess they felt that any sign of life from her was something to get thrilled about. Maybe they thought it would be the beginning of some kind of breakthrough for Lizzie, but it didn't happen—at least not as far as I could see. But for the next five years, they continued to talk about Lizzie's paintings with what was almost reverence.

For last five years of Lizzie's life, I began to block her out more than I had before. Not only was I embarrassed by her but now I felt ignored by the family because of her paintings. Lizzie had always required extra attention, but with her painting it seemed she was demanding even more. So for those five years, I became harsher in my attitude toward her. Whenever anything was said around the house about Lizzie, I acknowledged it even if I hadn't listened to what was said. I wanted any conversation about her to end as quickly as possible. I tried to make her as nonexistent to me as I was sure I was to her.

Mother and Father were devastated when Lizzie died, and though I did feel some remorse, the main emotion I felt was relief. At that time,

I was starting to keep company with young ladies. When Lizzie was no longer with us, I didn't have to feel embarrassed about bringing the young ladies home. Even back then, I knew I was being selfish, but for me it was better to feel a little guilt than the shame and embarrassment of being connected with Lizzie. But I was wrong and only realized it a few years later. By then the guilt had taken root, and once it did I was stuck with it.

I moved away from home about a year after Lizzie died. The escape from, or abandonment of, my family could have, under different circumstances, been fulfilled, but not for me. Because of Lizzie, a rift had developed between my parents and me; even her death could not traverse that chasm. I had turned my back on Lizzie; consequently, my parents turned their backs on me. They may not have done so completely, but, to a certain extent, they did. They never came right out and forbade me from coming home, but their attitude when I visited was very cold. They made it easy for me to stay away. They paid for my university education, and I had a trust fund for my other needs, which I used to travel frequently. I found it helped me to abandon the memories from my childhood.

As each year vanished into the past, I developed a whole life separate from my childhood and youth. Even before my parents died, I hadn't seen or talked to them for several years. I had gotten to the point where I had no desire to return to my childhood home. The only things that greeted me when I did go back a few times were the ghosts of Lizzie, and of my own guilt.

The last two occasions on which I returned to the town of my childhood were the separate funerals of my parents. Though Will had accepted a job after college in another state, he had returned home when our mother became gravely ill. The last time I saw Father alive, at Mother's funeral, he was still aloof to me, but I believe it was because of his loss and not the indiscretions of my youth. Will also told me at Mother's funeral that Father had seemed to lose interest in life, and he died shortly thereafter.

I found no reason to enter the house of my childhood after my father's death, so I left town immediately after the service and internment. Since Will had a life elsewhere and I had no desire to keep the house, selling it seemed the easiest and most logical solution. I didn't object to his decision and had no problem letting him having power of attorney over what was left of the estate. A part of me hoped the estate sale would vanquish the guilt I still held inside.

A few months after the funeral, I received a letter from Will. While going through the house in preparation for the estate sale, he had come across the paintings Lizzie had done as a child. They were part of a small group of items he wanted to keep. He had shown the paintings to a friend who worked at an art gallery in New York, and she showed interest in the paintings. Through connections, Will's friend was able to secure a showing of the paintings at a small art gallery in the city. Apparently what I had assumed to be products of doodling were actual paintings. Maybe if I had tried to care back then and looked closer at what Lizzie had painted, I could have been excited for her also. Enclosed in the letter was a brochure announcing the show and explaining a little bit about the artist. It seems our mother had kept a diary about Lizzie, and some excerpts from the diary were in the brochure.

From the time I received the letter from Will, a part of me knew I had to go to the exhibit. We all look for a means of redemption for the perceived sins of the heart. I had lived so long with the guilt of how I treated Lizzie as a child. But if truth be known, seeking redemption from guilt is a selfish act, especially in my case. Lizzie was dead. Trying to express how sorry I was catered to my own needs. It was the only way I could think of to deal with my guilt. Even if Lizzie had still been alive to tell her how wrong I had been, she couldn't have understood.

As much as I wanted to go to the opening night of the exhibition, I could not bring myself to do it. My main fear was that Will would point me out as the artist's brother. I wanted to view the paintings in solitude, not discuss my sister or my shame with others. I wasn't ready for that kind of scrutiny.

My curiosity was piqued by the third night of the exhibition when I decided to go. I had scanned over a few reviews after the opening night, and they all raved about the paintings. Some of them said the paintings were reminiscent of Monet's famous *Water Lily* masterpieces. I can't tell the difference between a Monet and a Manet, but those in the know were the ones with the best reviews.

Because Lizzie had finished only nine paintings, the exhibit was limited to a small side room of the gallery. An undercurrent of hushed murmurs cascaded through the room as I entered. I didn't strain to hear what was being said, but the feeling in the air was one of appreciation and astonishment.

Even though I had read the critic's reviews and was aware of their praise, which was not based on Lizzie's handicap but on the quality of her paintings, I was taken aback as soon as I looked at her work. They were definitely not some form of doodling. I had never been very interested in the painted art form, but from the first glance I could see there was something special about the paintings. And it had nothing to do with the fact that Lizzie spent her life in a catatonic state. After reading the critic's reviews, I went online and looked at some of the Monet's *Water Lily* paintings. It didn't make me an expert on art or anything, but, looking now at Lizzie's work, I could understand what the critics were talking about. I also felt something more than what the critics had discussed, and I understood what those feelings were. It all had to do with who Lizzie was as a girl and how I felt about and treated her while she was alive.

In the paintings I could see no acknowledgment of the shame or hurt that I (or others in society) had directed at her. There was nothing that portrayed the real world that most of us live in. In the world she knew there was no pain, no hatred, and no ugliness. There was only beauty and peace and tranquility. And as I looked at Lizzie's paintings, looked into her world, I was filled with happiness and comfort. I realized she never knew the real world that surrounded her. And, for the first time in my life, I cried for the sister I no longer had.

I Saw the Trees Move

"**B**ut the trees did move."

The man made one last feeble attempt to convince us his plight was real before he fell silent. He looked at us, his interrogators, as if hoping at last he would see in our faces a flicker of belief in his story. But his eyes were wild; the accumulation of ten grueling hours of interrogation had left him spent. I'm sure he wouldn't have recognized assent on our part unless all of us suddenly assured him we believed his story. Even then I'm not sure if it would have registered. He was now just a shell of a man teetering on the brink of insanity, a man who was probably wishing he could fall into that chasm of eternal nothingness and not have to fight with us or his own sanity any longer.

As the man was led from the room, I was overwhelmed by the feeling that our work here was of little consequence. The problem we faced had been with us for nearly three months. The phenomenon began slowly at first. A man and his wife had confronted the authorities on the west coast with a wild story about seeing trees move. The authorities had dismissed the validity of their claims; trees just don't move. They theorized the couple only thought they saw the trees move. It was only in their minds and not in reality, so they left them in the care of psychiatric professionals.

I am inclined to believe they were not the first to be affected by the phenomenon—only the first to report it. Most people, anticipating disbelief, wouldn't have said anything. But the eventuality of someone coming forward was inevitable.

As two more sightings were reported the following week and six the week after that, the local authorities finally contacted the government agency in which I worked. Although we weren't specifically organized to deal with strange or unexplained phenomena, we investigated them if they represented a possible threat to national security. Because we were certain more sightings were occurring than were being reported, we felt a larger problem existed.

One of the problems we faced from the start was the fact the media had learned of the situation as soon as we had. Our usual method of operation, when confronted with a situation we were unsure about, was to quarantine the area with a preplanned cover story. Usually that story credited a toxic spill if there were train tracks or a highway nearby. We had other stories for other circumstances. But because the media was on to the event from the start, we were unable to employ our usual plans when the sightings began. As more sightings appeared and the media's coverage followed every stage of them, our concern for mass hysteria only compounded the problem.

Our initial theory as to the cause of the problem was that some kind of mind-altering drug or virus had been introduced to the public, probably through the food or water supply. The agency had extensive information and experience in this area, for the government thought that, in this age, the greatest threat of warfare was biological or psychological. Not only would it be hard to combat but, if executed properly, it could be virtually impossible to verify the source—whether it was an individual nation or faction.

We were quickly able to verify that none of our country's facilities dealing in this area of research had experienced any kind of accident or sabotage. So we continued at first to think it was either from a hostile source or an extreme case of mass hysteria fueled by the media. But we could not find any evidence to support either of those theories. Usually, in cases of mass hysteria, a majority of the early affected individuals will have past histories or show evidence of psychotic behavior or (as funny as it sounds) extreme gullibility. But this was not the case, which became more evident as the sightings spread. We began to receive sightings from people who had not heard about it in the media and also from those in the professional field like police or psychiatrists.

So that left us with the theory that some new strain of virus or disease had infiltrated the public. But all our interrogations and examinations provided no evidence of either some type of brainwashing or a virus that was working on part of the brain. So we continued on with our work, though in actuality it wouldn't matter much longer. Already, sightings were appearing in other countries, and, at the rate of exponential increase, it would only be a matter of weeks before a majority of people were affected by the phenomenon.

As the door shut behind the man, I lowered my head and thought about his last statement. He may have been on the verge of insanity, but in those five simple words he was trying to convey to us a different perspective on the answers we sought. Through the course of the interrogation the man had been emphatic about one bit of information: he saw the trees move. It was a statement we thought we should be able to work with. If we could find what caused his brain to make him think he saw the trees move, then we could work on a way to cure him.

But as he realized what our questions meant, he tried to show us how to look at the problem. He was telling us that the trees actually moved. It was not important that he saw them move; the important thing was that they *did* move. He was removing the scrutiny from himself and throwing it back on us. If we were willing to believe what we had been sure was impossible, then we would have a better chance of finding a solution. Maybe some of the others we interrogated had tried to tell us the same thing, but we were unable to realize it before.

I am not ready to admit to the impossible. Even when I wake up in the morning, look in my mirror, and am greeted by such dark and shadowed eyes, I can't admit it. My eyes carry with them not only a look of fear and dread but—worst of all—realization. Today, when the man made his last feeble attempt to convince us, I saw the same look on my colleagues' faces that I see each morning on my own face in the mirror. The man was beyond the point where he could notice, but I did. My colleagues' faces stared back at me like the face in my mirror. I'm sure they knew what I knew, but to admit it was to admit insanity.

For, earlier this week, I saw the trees move. And like the man we just finished interrogating, it's not that I *thought* I saw the trees move; the trees *did* move.

The Long Stretch of Road

As we grow older, certain events and conversations from our past will forever stay with us. We know some will remain fresh in our memories because of the importance they had to us at the time they occurred. For example, I can remember a bad argument my parents had when I was a young boy. It sticks out because my parents rarely fought. I also remember the circumstances surrounding the day I lost my virginity. The night I went to a concert featuring my favorite musical group is also a vivid memory to me.

We also carry memories of things we wish we could forget. For me, it concerned something I did or said. At the time it happened, I thought it was going to be funny. But when we are young, we just don't think through our actions or words and only realize later what implications they might have. In retrospect, there are many such instances I regret and wish I could take back.

Fortunately the memory most vivid in my mind right now is not one that gives me feelings of regret. It is a memory that is more like a dream—so real I can't forget it. In fact, it was so out of the ordinary that I've been asking myself if maybe it wasn't really a dream at all. But more to the point, what if it was real and what was told to me is going to happen? What then?

The incident happened one night early last month as I was driving north through Nevada on my way home from Las Vegas. The sun was setting, as it does quickly over the vastness of the desert. While the darkness settled, I began to doze off. When the rumble strips along the shoulder of the highway woke me up, I decided it was time to pull to the side of the road and rest my eyes.

I'm not sure how long I slept, but suddenly I was fully awake, unaware of what had aroused me. I had the distinct feeling, however, that something had interrupted my sleep. For a few minutes I tried to reason what could have awakened me. There were no noises piercing the stillness of the night. I looked along the stretch of highway in both directions, but there were no lights from an advancing or receding car that could have aroused me. I couldn't even remember if I'd had a disturbing dream, so what awakened me remained a mystery.

I settled back into the car seat but found I was no longer sleepy. As I sat staring into the darkness, a feeling began to build within me. It was a feeling that there was something out in that darkness, something more than just the blackness. I felt compelled to discover what that something was.

Light sliced into the darkness as I opened the car door and stepped out. As I closed the door and began to walk, it never occurred to me to notice in what direction I was venturing. Time seemed not to matter as I walked. I was in a void, a fog, made up of an endless, stretching landscape of darkness. Gradually my eyes adjusted enough to the darkness so that I could distinguish the outlines of the boulders and small plants spread out along the desert floor. Finally I happened upon a road. It was an ordinary road, not unlike the road I had been traveling on, but I felt there was something different about it. As my eyes adjusted more to the dark I noticed the part of the road to my left was worn and dusty, showing evidence of cars having passed over it, while the part of the road to my right was clean. There were no tracks of any kind, and even the substance that comprised the road looked newer, as if it had been recently applied.

Another curious observation about the highway concerned the lane on the far side of the road. It was also clean; there were no tracks or dirt of any kind in either direction. I stood by the road, staring in bewilderment for some time, again feeling I was in a void where time didn't matter. My mind was confused by the differences in the road and what they could possibly mean. Could I be sleeping and dreaming the whole thing? That might explain the feeling that brought me here from the car or the peculiarities of the highway I was seeing. But I've heard this: if people wonder if they are dreaming, then they are not dreaming. If that is true, then I was awake.

An indefinite time later, the feeling intensified that there was someone or something else in the blackness of the desert. The feeling that made me leave the car in the first place had been forgotten over the peculiarities of the road, but it was back again. As I looked up from the pavement, I noticed a dim glow illuminating the sands and pavement in front of me. I could even make out my shadow as it fell across the highway. The increasing illumination behind me must have been what caused me to look up; it began to glow even brighter.

Fear flooded through me as I watched the glow intensify. If I was right about not dreaming and I had walked through the desert to this spot, then the glow behind me was real also. Did someone or something draw me out here? Was it now going to confront me? That thought scared me, so I tried to tell myself I was overreacting to the entire situation. There had to be a logical explanation to the peculiarities of the highway. Could I have possibly walked in circles and returned to the road I had been traveling on earlier? Maybe the light coming from behind me was from the flashlight of a patrolman who had noticed my empty car by the side of the road. I found I was really hoping that was the case.

As these thoughts flowed through my mind, a noise began to accompany the glow behind me. The sound was unintelligible, and yet there was something familiar about it. Growing in volume, just as the glow had increased in brightness, I realized it wasn't only one sound I was hearing but a mixture of many sounds. I could hear voices—both laughing and crying. Some of the voices were whispering while others were yelling, but I couldn't make out any of the words. Other sounds assaulted my ears along with the voices. There were sounds like running vehicles, beating noises like hammers striking metal, and what sounded like bombs exploding. The noises were becoming too intense, and I was about to cover my ears with my hands when the sounds greatly subsided.

"Turn around, and look upon me," a voice from behind me said over the murmur of noises.

My original fear, momentarily replaced by curiosity about the noises, flooded back through me. But there was something about the voice that confused me. The voice was commanding, and I knew I would not be able to refuse it. At the same time, it had a sweet, gentle tone, and I felt that whoever (or whatever) the voice belonged to would not harm me. As much as I felt this to be true and could almost guarantee it, I was still filled with trepidation. With a wildly beating heart, I turned to see who had addressed me.

The light was so bright that I had to shield my eyes. I waited for the voice to speak again, but all that penetrated the silence of the desert was the continuous cacophony of noises that seemed to come from the core of the brightness. Maybe my eyes began to adjust to the light or maybe the light dimmed, for as I waited for something to happen, I began to distinguish some kind of shape at the very center of the light.

"Take your hands away from your face, and look upon me. There is much for you to see."

I lowered my hand, and the sight that displayed itself filled me with wonder and awe. As I had already noticed, there appeared to be a shape from which the light was being emitted. But now, as I looked at the shape, it took on even more of a form. The shape appeared to be some kind of robed or shrouded figure. It didn't appear to be made up of flesh or anything solid—just some kind of a mist or vapor that was continually in motion. It looked like the shrouded figure one moment; the next moment it possessed no particular shape at all.

The mist was dazzling in brilliance of the purest colors I've ever seen. They seemed to float on the mist. As I looked at the figure, I felt I was looking at something completely good and perfect, better than anything I could ever describe. I have never seen anything so beautiful in my life, and I almost had to turn away because I felt if I looked at it much longer, I might never be able to take my eyes off it. At the same time, I was more afraid than I have ever been, and a sickness pulsed in my stomach, head, and every joint in my body.

As the mist swirled around the figure, I occasionally caught glimpses of utter grotesqueness just behind the façade of the mist. I saw terrible wars and naked, bloodied, crying children. There were people whose flesh was melting away from their bones. There were other scenes assaulting my senses so horrible that I can't find words to describe them. But these scenes were mere glimpses, so I was caught between wanting to see the beautiful and repulsed by the hideous.

"What do you see?" the voice asked.

My natural inclination was to look to where the figure's eyes should have been, but only the swirling vapors greeted me. I opened my mouth to speak but couldn't find what I wanted to say. Confusion displaced my curiosity. What was I seeing and how could I really explain it?

"Why don't you speak?" the voice continued.

I finally found my voice. "I don't know what I see. What are you?"

"I am another entity that exists in time."

I was silent for a moment, trying to comprehend what I had just been told, but I remained as confused as before. I had never believed in ghosts or extraterrestrial beings, but they were the first two thoughts that came to mind. Could this be the spirit of someone who had died in the past or an alien from another planet? I just didn't know.

"Are you confused?" the entity asked.

"Yes."

"Then I shall try to explain to you in terms you can understand. Like you, I am an entity that exists in the realm of this earth. My kind is compelled by the same emotions as your kind. We are restricted on this earth by many of the same conditions. We think and feel and live a lot like you do, but we are different in that we have no body of flesh and bones to restrict our movements. We are made up of experiences and memories of the past and of hopes and dreams of the future. We can control our thoughts and emotions to focus only that which is good."

"Are you from the future then?" Increasingly I was feeling that this entity, whatever it was, would not harm me, and in that hope I found courage to speak more freely.

"No. My kind lives on this earth along with you. In the realm of time and space there are many dimensions. Many forms of living beings can and do live in the same space and time but in different, shall we say, dimensions. Some of your scientists are just now learning there are ways for objects to occupy the same space in different dimensions, but that is not important for you to know.

"In the beginning, we were humans—just as you are—and progressed along a similar evolutionary path. But over many centuries we came to realize how restricted we were by having human bodies. So we gradually developed to the form in which we now exist. Your path of humanity just took a different route. Though we exist in another sphere of space that normally makes us invisible to you, we do exist in the same sphere of time. We know of other races of humanity and surmise there could be innumerable races of humankind. From time to time, we have made ourselves known to your kind."

"But what is it I see when I look at you?"

"What you see is not a being made up of solid matter but rather a form of matter made up of memories and emotions. The shadow of a shape you see is the shape in which we once existed, the shape you still possess. The noises you hear and the sights you see are the memories from our past and the hopes for our future. We are enveloped in what is good and pure; evil no longer exists within us. But within us are the memories of the days when we were not pure. It is by these memories that we learn to live, knowing what mistakes we should not repeat."

"If you're perfect, why do you need the memories about what is evil and wrong?"

"I never said we were perfect; I said we were pure. We live—"

"What's the difference?" I was becoming more confused. "Aren't purity and perfection the same things?"

"We live in a state of purity; evil does not exist in us, and we live without sin. But we are not perfect. We still have the ability in us to commit sins and let evil back into our lives. That is why we are filled with the memories of the past—to remind us what would happen should we fail and allow evil to overcome us."

"Okay." I still wasn't completely sure if I understood what the entity was saying or if I ever would. I decided to try a different approach. "So why are you here?"

"I am here to explain to you the meaning of this road."

The statement flooded my mind with its own possibilities. First, the road was not an ordinary road, though I had pretty much come to that conclusion already, and it was somehow here because of the entity. Second, the entity might be able to read my thoughts and knew I was confused by the road. I'm not sure if I liked the idea of someone (or something) being able to read my thoughts, but it was the least of my worries at the moment.

I turned sideways so that I could look back and forth from the entity to the road. I had been drawn into the desert for a reason. This entity had somehow brought me to see this highway and explain to me its meaning. But why had I been picked? Why should I be afforded knowledge normally out of the reach of most?

"What do you see in front of you?"

"I see a road."

"You have just committed a mistake that has plagued most of your kind since your history began. You look only with your eyes, so you see only what is on the surface. Before you can find answers, you must be able to ask the right questions; before you can ask the right questions, you must be able to look at life intelligently. Look with your heart and your mind, as well as your eyes. Let your eyes be the mechanism to relay to your mind information to be processed. Don't look only for the outcome of happenings but also for the meanings, for the reasons things exist. Now tell me what you see."

I looked at the highway again and thought about what the entity had said. I tried, but I could not find any meaning to the complexities of the road. "I see a road that stretches as far as I can see in both directions. It's been recently paved from this point, and not many cars travel in the far lane."

I thought of what else I might say, but there was nothing more I could see, so I stood silently peering at the road.

"You look harder, but still you look only with your eyes. You try not to reason why the road is the way it is but only that it is. You are looking at it the wrong way."

"If you are here to explain to me the meaning of the road, why must we play this game? Just tell me what it means."

I began to tremble as I finished speaking. The entity had been friendly to me thus far, but I hadn't raised my voice or made any action that might be construed as threatening. Might it take my yelling as a form of hostility? If so, what might it do?

"You are a good example of your kind." The entity spoke in the same tone of voice as before, as if it didn't fear my hostility or hadn't sensed my anger or didn't care. "You are not patient when looking for answers, if you even venture to look for them. You don't try to change the world you live in; you just try to exist. There are those among you who are trying to make your world better and others who are destroying your world. But you are like the majority. You take what is given you and want others to do the work."

"But I don't see the meaning of the road. I'm sorry, but I just don't see it."

I was becoming desperate now. What the entity had said hit a chord inside me. I knew I was the type of person it described, always leaving problems and decisions to others and finding a way to live with the solutions they came up with. This wasn't the case in my personal life. All of us have to make decisions on some matters, though some of us aren't even good at that. But in the general world we exist with the rules others have set.

I really wanted to see the meaning of the road. I felt what the entity was trying to show me was important; why else would it be here? I was trying, but there just wasn't anything there I could see. Like most people, I needed someone to show me the way and lead me.

"The highway represents the path of humankind. To your left is the path from where humankind has come, and to your right is the future toward which your kind is traveling. That is why the tracks only go to the point at which you stand. That is the extent to which humankind has traveled."

The entity fell silent as I looked at the highway. I guess what the entity was saying made sense, but I didn't know how it expected me to figure that out for myself. I wondered what would happen if I stepped onto the highway. When I first noticed the entity, I stepped back a little from the highway, so now there were about five feet between the road and me. I took a step forward, expecting the entity to tell me to stop, but all I heard were the voices and noises that surrounded the entity. As I advanced closer to the highway, the sounds from the entity subsided, and when I finally stepped onto the highway, the noises ceased altogether and were replaced by new sounds.

I staggered momentarily as a powerful gust of wind whipped around me. When I regained my balance, I tried to discern what was happening. A fog was being buffeted about by the wind, and my first thought was that this must be the kind of existence the entity lived in. I turned around to look at the entity, but the fog had surrounded me completely, and I could not see through it. Just as I had seen forms and events in the mist around the entity, I began to get quick glimpses of people through the swirling fog. I strained to see who they were. I was surprised to see myself and others I had been with during the previous day or two. I could see spending time in the casinos in Las Vegas, driving along the highway here, and walking through the darkness of the desert to this very spot. These same glimpses repeated themselves over and over.

I stepped back the way I had come (or thought I had come) and found myself standing by the side of the road again. When I turned back to the road, it looked the same as before; it wasn't wider or longer or older. It was the same, yet I felt different; I cannot say exactly how though. The glimpses I witnessed made me think how things from the past are never forgotten. I had seen what happened to me in the last day or so, as if it was still happening. Maybe, in a sense, it was. Maybe the lives of people relived themselves over and over in different spheres. The same people laughed and cried, loved and hated. And they made the same mistakes over and over. That's what bothered me the most—the mistakes and wrongs I had done would never be forgotten. Somewhere my sins would always be remembered. Maybe that was what the entity was trying to show me: we must learn from our mistakes.

If the part of the road to my left carried the memories of my past, could the road to my right hold the answers to my future? I took a few steps to my right, but as I did, the tire tracks and worn appearance on the pavement inched forward, staying even with me. The entity said nothing when I turned and looked at it, so I turned back and took a step onto the highway. Again the wind and swirling fog surrounded me. I looked for the tiny glimpses I knew I would get and was surprised when the glimpses also revealed the moments just before I stepped onto the highway. I could see myself walking back and forth along the highway and looking at the entity. The entity began to speak as I stepped back out into the desert night.

"You will always be able to see that which has happened, for it is comprised of the memories of the past. It cannot be changed. But as for the future, it is something you cannot see until it happens. If you could see your future, it would show the choices you are to make—the choices you haven't yet made. That is where the far side of the highway comes into meaning."

I looked at the far lane of the highway and thought about what the entity had said. "So that lane has something to do with our choices?"

"Now you are beginning to look with more than just your eyes. You are looking with your heart and soul because you really wish to know the answers. The far lane does deal with choices. It represents the choices humans have not made, the paths they have not chosen. And it is because of that lane that the future can never be known. But we all can have a hand in the direction the future may take."

For the first time, the tone of the entity's voice changed in pitch, and I looked deeper into the swirling mist. The glow from the entity vibrated in density, and I wondered if the changes in the glow indicated emotion. The tone in which the entity had spoken made me feel as though it possessed some deep knowledge.

"What do you mean, we can direct the future?"

Though I knew humans played a part in the earth's history I felt the entity meant something more.

As the entity began to speak again its glow diminished back to its earlier state. "Because humans have free will and the ability to make decisions, they can make decisions that will affect the future of not only themselves but all living beings. Humans can build bombs not only for protection but also for the ultimate destruction of the world. They can build proud and beautiful cities, but in the process they will rape the land, leaving it barren and desolate. Humans cannot know for sure what the future holds, but to a certain extent they can dictate it.

"And that is why I have shown myself to you today. Humanity is destroying the world around them. If this thoughtless evil leads to the ultimate destruction of your kind, it will lead to the ultimate destruction of all living beings, including those who are like me.

"Look back at the road. The path by which you have come is laden with memories. Learn by the mistakes you have made. Think about the results of your decisions. Now look at the path of the future. It is clean.

No future has yet been set. You can control what will happen. You can pave the way to a better tomorrow. Don't let your world be destroyed."

I continued to look at the highway after the entity finished speaking. A deep feeling of dread stirred in the pit of my stomach. I knew what the entity said was true. Humans were destroying the world in which they lived. But was the entity right about the future? Could humans change what they appeared to be heading toward? Could they control what was to come?

"But if, as you say, the future cannot be known for sure, then maybe what you fear will not come about."

The entity replied, "Though no one can tell with certainty what the future holds, my kind does have the ability to discern possible outcomes. There are many possible paths your kind may take; many of them lead to destruction. As time goes by and changes aren't made, the chances of destruction increase."

There were so many other questions I wanted to ask, so many things I wasn't sure about. Just as I was about to speak, I noticed the entity was glowing brighter again. "But why pick me?" I asked quickly, fearing the entity was preparing to leave.

"We have been revealing ourselves to many members of your race. Each of you will face crucial decisions in the near future that may have profound effects on the destiny of humankind. We did not want to interfere; we hoped we wouldn't have to, but we decided we can't be observers any longer. Even with our appearance and giving you knowledge of what may happen, we are sure some of you will choose not to heed our warnings. We've looked at all possible outcomes and the chances of each of them happening, and yet the future may still be lost. That's why it's imperative you take heed of what we say and make your decisions accordingly."

The glow from the entity continued to build until it was the same brilliance I had first witnessed, and yet it continued to glow brighter. I put my hands to my eyes, but it seemed not to matter because the light came right through the flesh of my hands. I was becoming dizzy and began to lose consciousness. Before I blacked out, I heard the entity speak once more.

"Time is growing short. Every human has a part to play but few realize their importance. Heed my words; do it for your sake, our sakes, and for the sake of every form of life."

I opened my eyes and saw the dashboard of my car, unsure of how I got back to my car after I blacked out. Maybe the entity brought me back. And then again, maybe the whole episode had just been a dream or some kind of hallucination. I stepped out of the car and looked at the sand for prints. Though I could see my prints as I walked around—both leaving the car and returning—no other prints accented the desert floor.

So that is the incident that happened to me, one that has weighed heavily on my mind since. I have nothing to prove it wasn't a dream, but somehow I know it wasn't. And would it matter even if it was? We all know the dangers we are facing. And it doesn't matter if my subconscious told me these things while dreaming, what matters is whether or not I do anything about what I was told. I don't know how much I can dictate or control. I don't know how much I can direct the future, but I have to try. The only hope is that I, and others like me, will act.

Humans have brought us this far, and only humans will guide us into the future.

Stop the Whispers

What makes someone morally conscientious? Why do so many of us feel the need to help and comfort our fellow human beings? As a society we hold the notion that we are expected to help those in need, to care for their well-being. But how far are we expected to carry out this help and care for others? Some people go to extremes and are known as heroes. But for most of us, is there a point where it's all right for us to stop? Shouldn't we consider our own well-being first? In our everyday lives we usually don't have to consider such questions.

I have always considered my life to be average. I am not a standout in my profession. I am not famous. Outside of my family and friends I am not well known, and when I die, my name will go with me to be eventually forgotten. I am neither rich nor poor, and, like so many others, I struggle at times to pay the bills. I am interchangeable with a vast majority of the population. And, like so many others, there are aspects of my past that involve unchangeable regrets—things I wish had happened differently. People might forget many things over the course of their lives, but regrets stay with them until they die. And the memories of regrets can be triggered by so many different things.

I heard "Maggie May" by Rod Stewart the other day, and it made me think of a foster sister I had when I was a young boy. For years, my mother and father were foster parents, so, as a child, I had a number of foster brothers and sisters. Some of the kids were with us for just a day or two, while some were with us for years. I remember many of their names and get glimpses in my mind of their faces, but I'm sure I've forgotten some of them. However, I'll always remember Donna. She was with us the longest—over five years. In many ways I thought of her as a real sister.

One Christmas I gave Donna a Rod Stewart 45 rpm single. The funny thing is it wasn't even "Maggie May"; it was "Tonight's the Night." But still, hearing "Maggie May" caused me to think of Donna and that Christmas.

Recalling Donna and Christmas and Rod Stewart conjured up some other emotions. Part of it was definitely nostalgia. I look at nostalgia in a good light, a yearning for a simpler time before the demands of the world invaded life. The Rod Stewart song filled me with nostalgia. But memories can also carry strong feelings of pain or dread or sadness. And my nostalgia turned to sadness as a news brief followed the song.

The report told about a search being conducted for a seven-year-old boy who had gotten separated from his Boy Scout troop while hiking through a state wilderness preserve. Listening to it, the story sent chills through me for more than one reason. A parent's worst fear is a child becoming lost. Fortunately my children are all grown now, but I am still concerned for my children and the well-being of their families. But I no longer have that abject terror waiting in the back of my mind of one of them becoming lost.

I had lost track of my daughter one time at the beach when she was little. The fear I had during those few minutes before she was found playing in the sand along the shoreline was unlike anything I can even begin to describe. She had no idea anything was wrong and was probably too young to completely understand what was happening.

But when she saw how upset her mother and I were, she started to cry. I guess it's true what they say: it's possible to sometimes scare someone with too much love.

The incident with my daughter is a strong and powerful memory, and it was natural for me to remember it when hearing of the lost boy. But what also came back to me, with the suddenness and unexpectedness of a thunderclap in the dark of night, was the memory of Tom Mutton. Tom didn't play a very important part in my life; I can't even say he was ever a friend. *Acquaintance* is a more accurate description. He was a classmate of mine one fall semester at the small college I attended in the upper peninsula of Michigan. Tom was just one of the many nondescript students roaming the campus, as I probably was to him. I'm sure I had seen him around, but his was just another face in the crowd, at least until one early autumn Saturday. His actions on that day allowed the whole college to learn a name to go along with the face. The next day his anonymity vanished.

It had been a quiet Sunday morning on campus. It was an academic college I was attending, so even though it was fall, we had no football team to preoccupy students. There were a few labs being conducted on campus and a few clubs some students attended, but on the weekends most students either stayed in their rooms studying or hung out with friends on campus or in the small town nearby. It wasn't a normal college town, but it held enough interest for us because, as students, we didn't come to the college for the party life or any extracurricular activities.

I had spent a leisurely morning reading a letter from my parents and had begun to write one back to them. I didn't enjoy writing letters, so I didn't get too far. My attention kept being diverted out the window because it was turning into a nice, inviting autumn day. Knowing that colder and damper weather would soon be the norm, I wanted to enjoy any nice weather that was left in the year. There had already been a few short, cold spells; the previous day and night had been cold, wet, and dreary. The sun was already burning off some of the dew that clung to the ground, so I decided to take a walk through some of the trails in the woods that bordered the campus. Even before I left the dorm, I could sense that there was something different in the air. (Sometimes a person can just feel it without any visible signs to back up the feeling.) There were always groups of people talking among themselves; by outward appearances the day shouldn't have felt different from any other, but it did.

As I left the dormitory, I observed even more groups of people talking than usual. My curiosity was really piqued, and I wondered what I was missing.

"Hey, Danny."

The voice startled me; I believe I even jumped a little. I turned to see my friend Andrea smiling as she walked toward me. I considered Andrea to be a good/close friend. Attending college, regardless of the size of the institution, one had a lot of acquaintances: classmates and others who lived in the dormitory. They were students to speak to casually, without knowing their names. One might glimpse fragments of people's personalities by talking to them but not enough to have them become part of one's inner circle. Besides, who really knows why or how we pick certain people to become close friends, while others remain at arm's length. But Andrea was one of those people I allowed into my inner circle, and I spent more time with her on campus than with anyone else.

My first thought was to ask Andrea if she would like to go hiking with me. I knew she frequented the trails, and I had been on many hikes with her in the past. Seeing Andrea almost made me forget the feeling I had that something was a little out of the ordinary.

"Hey, Andi, what's up?"

"It's kind of crazy, isn't it? I mean, it's good what happened, but I'd be freaking out if it happened to me."

It only took a second for Andrea to realize by the look on my face that I had no idea what she was talking about. "You mean, you haven't heard?"

"Heard what? What's going on?"

"Where have you been the past day?"

I liked Andrea a lot, and she was a dear friend, but she had the annoying habit of answering a question with another question. It could be a struggle sometimes to get information out of her. I could have told her how I had gone for a drive the previous day to think some things through, and it had been late when I returned. My roommate had gone away for the weekend, and he was one of those, besides Andrea, who kept me in the loop of current events on campus. Instead of explaining, I just gave her my best "quit messing with me" look.

"I can't believe you haven't heard. Everyone's talking about—"

"And I'm wondering if I'm ever going to find out anything from you." I was serious in my comment, but I was trying to say it in a voice whereby Andrea wouldn't think I was getting annoyed with her. When I ended my statement with a sly smile, Andrea burst out in laughter.

"I'm doing it again, aren't I, Danny?"

This time Andrea was the one to give a sly smile, and I was the one to laugh.

"Anyway, Tom Mutton went out yesterday for a jog to Bluffton's Point, and while he was jogging, he came across a lost little boy. Apparently the boy had walked out of his house and into the woods when no one was looking. I don't know all the details, but what I've heard is that he lives over by the elementary school in town, and Tom found him about a quarter mile from Bluffton's Point. That's almost five miles from his home. The boy didn't have a coat on, and you know how damp and cold it was yesterday and last night. He had been missing for several hours before anyone realized it. The police were just setting up a search party when they got word the boy had been found.

"And it was a lucky thing. The police think they probably would have only been able to cover a one-to-two-mile radius of territory before darkness set in. If Tom hadn't found the boy, the police were pretty sure they wouldn't have found him until the next day. By then it might have been too late. When Tom found him, he was already in the first stages of hypothermia. Tom saved the boy. He's a hero."

And so he was. The story was already circulating around campus, but it didn't stop there. Within days the local newspaper wrote a small article about the incident. Eventually both the major papers in Michigan and Wisconsin wrote more in-depth articles, and the Associated Press wrote a feel-good story that ran in many papers across the country.

For the rest of that fall and into the winter, Tom Mutton remained a popular figure on campus. People went out of their way to talk to him and try to get him to join their clubs or cliques. I'll even admit that I talked to him a little more than before, but it was out of respect for what he did. I didn't pretend I wanted him for a new friend. Besides, anyone who was really observant could see that Tom was uncomfortable with all the attention he was getting. Fortunately for him, our society is very superficial. Before winter was over, most people on campus had either forgotten about Tom's achievement or found other things to occupy their thoughts and time.

I do remember seeing Tom walking by himself a few times as winter turned into spring. Just a few months earlier, at the height of his popularity, he was never seen walking around campus by himself. Occasionally I saw Andrea with him. She had been his friend—the only one I really knew of—before he had his fifteen minutes of fame, and she remained true in her friendship when all the others forgot about him.

Eventually he simply disappeared from the campus. I'll admit I can't say when that happened; I was more like the others than like Andrea. But there was more to the story of Tom Mutton's life than I remembered from that autumn on campus. It was through Andrea that I would hear the whole story.

I wasn't overly surprised when Andrea contacted me recently and asked if I would accompany her to a funeral. We weren't as close as we'd been in high school and college. However, we had always stayed in contact over the years, setting up a routine where we alternated a trip each year to the other's home town for an extended weekend visit. And through the high school class reunions we attended, we had stayed as close as possible. Technology had also helped our friendship. We had telephones all along, but with the advent of personal computers and advanced smart phones we used emails and text messages to communicate. So even though our relationship may not have been as close as it once had been, it was definitely closer than most childhood friendships remain over time.

We had attended each other's wedding and had been a caring and sympathetic ear for each other when divorce hit each of us in turn. Overall we had remained close, but I still felt we were drifting away from each other as each year passed. So I was happy when I answered my cell phone and heard her voice. I should have known it was more than just a friendly call because, more times than not, it was the emails or text messages she used to converse with me; phone conversations we saved for more important or personal news. We exchanged pleasantries, and then she asked me to accompany her to a funeral.

When she told me whose funeral it was, a plethora of memories flooded through me. I had not thought of Tom Mutton for many years, but I would never forget him or the autumn when he made his mark on this earth. Little did I realize the extent of his impact on other people. Andrea needed to share with someone the secret she knew about Tom; that was one of the reasons she asked me to attend the funeral with her.

It had been almost eight months since Andrea and I had seen each other. Although we were to meet in a location away from where either of us lived, we arranged it so we could spend a couple of days together after the funeral. Andrea picked me up from the airport early on the morning of the funeral because it was to be held in a small town, and the nearest airport was about fifty miles away. Though I was curious about what Andrea wanted to tell me, she seemed subdued as she drove. We only exchanged small talk during the drive.

I noticed two things as we pulled into the church parking lot. First, I was surprised by how few cars were there. The service was supposed to start soon, so a majority of the people attending should already have arrived. I've seen in movies or in TV shows where only a handful of people attend a funeral, but all the funerals I'd been to were always well attended. And Tom hadn't been that old; he was around Andrea's and my age, so I thought there would have been more friends and family present. As I thought about his age, I wanted to ask Andrea how he died. I wondered if it was an accident or an illness of some kind.

My wonder about that was quickly replaced with confusion when I noticed the sign in front of the church announcing funeral services for a Richard Smith. The date and time indicated the service for him corresponded with the service for Tom, which Andrea and I were supposed to attend.

"Uh, Andi, are you sure we're at the right place?" I had not taken my eyes off the sign as we pulled in to the lot, so Andrea must have seen where I was looking.

"Yes, Danny, I'm sure. There's a lot I need to explain to you about Tom, but I wanted to wait until after the service. Let me just say that Richard Smith is really Tom Mutton. When I tell you what I need to, you'll understand why he changed his name."

Usually when I wanted to get some information from Andrea or she was trying to keep secrets from me, it wouldn't take much prodding for her to start talking. But there was something in her voice that stopped me from pursuing the matter. She sounded sad, somber, and tired all at the same time. I had been with Andrea through many events in her life, both good and bad, and I had never seen her quite this way. A simple *okay* was the only answer I gave Andrea as she parked the car.

Walking in silence toward the doors of the small church I slipped my hand over hers. She instantly readjusted her hand so that she could slip her fingers between mine. Andrea was not one who liked to be touched in public. I remembered she didn't even want to hold hands with a boyfriend she had in college, so to grasp my hand the way she did made me wonder even more what was bothering her.

The casket was in the foyer of the small church. I remembered the incident with Tom Mutton, but as I looked at the figure in the casket, I realized I had forgotten what he looked like. As is so often the case, the years had eroded the features of someone known from the past until all that was left was a name and a shadowy image. I had thought about Tom after Andrea called. I could remember incidents that involved him, but I now realized I only knew it was Tom from memory; the figure in my recollections had been nondescript. But the figure in the casket was definitely Tom. I recognized him, and I could picture in my mind how he had looked in college. The years had changed his appearance quite a bit, as it does to most of us, and he had that waxen look of the dead.

After a moment of paying respects, Andrea leaned toward me and told me to go inside and get us a seat in one of the pews. Then, after retracting her hand from mine, she moved toward an older couple who were standing about five feet to the side of the casket. As I headed toward the center of the church, I watched as Andrea greeted the couple. It dawned on me that the couple must be Tom's parents. I couldn't hear the greetings and condolences Andrea gave to them, but I had the impression she already knew them. It made me wonder how well Andrea had known Tom.

As she took her seat beside me, Andrea again slid her hand into mine. We sat silently through the short service. I listened to what was being said, but my thoughts were still fixed on what it was Andrea wanted to tell me. Tom was being interned at the back of the small cemetery next to the church. A few cars followed the hearse to his final resting place; Andrea and I joined the other attendees walking to the site. After the final words from the minister, Andrea again spoke with Tom's parents for a few minutes, and then we left the cemetery.

One of my faults is my lack of patience, especially when I want to find out something I'm sure someone else knows. I was ready to learn what Andrea wanted to tell me, but her mood kept me from pursuing the matter. I knew she needed to tell me, but it would be better if I let her do so in her own time, in her own way. I know that sometimes it takes me a while to find the right words to express something; if I'm hurried, I don't really use the right words or use them the way I want to. Maybe this was the quandary Andrea found herself in.

I remained silent as Andrea drove the car away from the cemetery. She had reserved some rooms for us at a hotel near the airport, and I wondered if the drive back would be in silence. As much as I had looked forward to visiting with Andrea, what I felt now was awkwardness. The silence was becoming a burden as we went back through the heart of the small town where the funeral had taken place. I was just about ready to speak (my patience was wearing thin) when Andrea steered the car into the parking lot of a cafe.

Looking at the small building, I was filled with nostalgia and a sense of comfort. Most cities of any real size are now populated with modern restaurant chains: Appleby's, TGI Fridays, Buffalo Wild Wings, and the like. I enjoy going to those restaurants at times; they have some really good-tasting food, but there is something impersonal about them. In small towns, where food chains have not invaded, the small diners and cafes still thrive.

Andrea seemed to be a little more upbeat as we exited the car and walked toward the doors of the diner. She smiled and asked if I was hungry. I smiled back, answered yes, and then silence surrounded us again as we entered the diner and found a table. Instantly, that comfortable, relaxed feeling overtook me, especially when the waitress came and treated us like long-time friends or family. I hoped this would soothe Andrea enough to finally open up to me. I was right, for she began to talk to me as soon as we placed our orders for drinks, and the waitress moved away from our table.

"So, how much do you remember about Tom?"

"Do you mean Tom, or do you mean Richard?"

"Yeah, I guess that does need an explanation. Like I said before, Tom legally changed his name. He hoped it would help him forget about his past in some way. I don't think it worked. You'll understand when you know everything. So again, what do you remember about Tom?"

"Well, I didn't really know him that well. I mean, I do remember him from college, and, to be honest with you, that is only because of his fifteen minutes of fame. I can't say I would've remembered him at all if it hadn't been for that."

"He did make quite an impression on everyone that fall, didn't he?"

"He sure did. He dropped below the radar pretty quick after that though. I remember he was quite shy, so he had to be uncomfortable with all that attention. That's pretty much all I remember. I might have gone the rest of my life without giving him another thought if you hadn't called me. Apparently there is something more you want to tell me about him."

As I finished speaking, the waitress stopped at our table to drop off our drinks and take our orders. As had happened so often over the years, one of Andrea's stories was once again to be delayed. But this time it wasn't her fault. At first I didn't feel the annoyance I had felt often during college, but as I waited for Andrea to decide what she wanted to eat my curiosity increased, and my patience waned. What had caused her to ask me to the funeral? I was sure there was more to it than just wanting my support. When Andrea finally gave her meal order, I quickly added mine and then waited for the waitress to leave. Only Andrea could put me on edge like this.

"I can't wait to eat. I didn't have an appetite earlier and didn't think I would today at all, but now that the service for Tom is over, I do feel a little better." Andrea paused for a moment, and I was about to tell her I was ready to know what she wanted to tell me when she spoke again. "That wasn't the only time Tom found a child."

Her statement caused a kind of chill to run down my spine. It wasn't really how she said it; I knew intuitively there was a lot more to it than her simple statement. Could it be just a coincidence that he had saved more than one child?

"So he saved another child? That's a good thing, isn't it? How come you never said anything about it before?"

There were so many questions popping into my head after her statement, but then I realized I was the one stopping her from telling her story. When she started talking again, I decided not to interrupt her.

"There's a lot about Tom that even I didn't know for a long time. He always said I was his best friend, and I guess, in the way he looked at it, I was. But it was nothing like what you and I had."

Although I was intensely interested in what Andrea had to say about Tom, I was struck by her use of the word *had*.

She continued, "As far as I know, I was the closest friend he ever had. We didn't go out chumming or anything like that, but we all need someone to talk to at times, and he picked me for that. What he told me, what I learned about him, has nagged at me for years. Now that he is gone, I want to share it with you. It's always felt, oh, I don't know, like when you don't feel good, and you wish you could get rid of whatever is making you feel that way. I know telling you won't take it away, but I think it will make me feel better."

"What?"

"Please, Danny, let me finish. Let me get it all out while I know what I want to say and tell it to you as I remember it."

I was flabbergasted. Andrea was cutting me off so that she could tell her story quicker. No interruptions for her. It was just as well, since I couldn't get out the words I wanted to use.

"The truth is I don't know how many kids he saved. I do know of four, two because he told me about them, one because I witnessed it, and the one you know about. There might have been more. He did say the first one was that fall at college, the one you're aware of."

The waitress stopped for a moment as she passed our table to tell us our sandwiches were just about ready. So Andrea paused in her narrative and took a sip of her iced tea as she waited for the waitress to move on. I knew Andrea wanted to tell her story her way, but I couldn't help but ask a question.

"You said it was only kids he found? That seems a little strange. I mean adults get lost too. I guess it's good at least that he was helping kids. I don't know; it just seems weird to me."

Andrea was about to put the glass back down on the table, but when I spoke, she hesitated for a moment and then took another sip of the tea before setting the glass down.

"I hope I can explain this right so that you'll understand. Yes, it was always kids he helped. That's one of the things that made it so difficult for me; it breaks my heart when I hear about children in trouble. It always has. This is the strange part: Tom told me how he could hear the thoughts of children when they were in distress. I know how it sounds, but in time I grew to believe him, and he proved it, as far as I'm concerned. But that part's for later.

"Tom said it was that fall when he began to understand what was going on. He had started to hear voices in his head that summer, but they were jumbled; he couldn't even tell if they were really voices. And they were infrequent. He thought it might be an after-effect of the bout of meningitis he suffered that spring. I believe what happened to him might have been caused by that; a part of his brain was triggered or unlocked or affected … somehow."

Our food arrived at that point, so there was a lull in her story. The aroma from my food made me realize how hungry I really was, so I readily started eating. But Andrea seemed to have lost her appetite. After a few small bites, she just fidgeted with her food. Reliving the past really seemed to be affecting her.

"Anyway, during the fall you remember he went out for a jog to get away from the other students on campus. As he got deeper into the woods, he thought he could hear a little boy's voice somewhere off in the distance. That was one of the reasons he took the trail that led to Bluffton's Point. It was the direction he was sure the voice was coming from. As he continued along the trail, he could tell he was getting closer to the boy because the voice was getting louder, but it seemed he might be circling the boy because he was searching for such a long time. At first the words were a little garbled because of the distance, but even then he could sense the fear and confusion in the tone of the voice. It was actually making him feel sick to his stomach. He said it reminded him of a time when he was at the scene of a bad car accident. He didn't see it happen but heard it—the loud screech of tires locking up and the awful sound of metal crashing into metal. It was so loud that the whole time he was running to the scene he felt sick to his stomach because the sound of the accident made him think that someone had to be seriously hurt, if not dead. He felt nauseous that day from thinking he was going to see something he really didn't want to see.

"Another thing that distressed him was when he got close enough to begin making out the words, they didn't make a lot of sense. He said the words themselves were okay—like *mother, where, lost,* and *help*—but they were mixed together, not in sentences. But he could tell what the boy meant. And more than that, he could feel what the boy was going through. What he felt made Tom rush even faster to find the boy."

The whole time Andrea was talking she continued to nibble at her sandwich. Even after I finished eating, she continued taking small bites every now and then, so the waitress left us pretty much alone, stopping by only once to replenish our drinks.

"Tom started to call out to the boy and knew then that he was close because the boy began to yell for him. But Tom said everything really started to get more jumbled then. He could hear the boy yelling for him, but it was mixed with the voice he heard originally, and he realized then that the voices were separate from each other, though they were from the same person. And the feelings he experienced while hearing the first voice were even stronger as he got closer to the boy. It wasn't long before he found the boy. He realized later that what led him to the boy wasn't the voice but what he was feeling inside. It acted as a guide.

"After he found the boy, he figured out that not only could he hear the boy when he spoke but he was also hearing his thoughts and feeling his emotions. He didn't reflect on that for long, for he could see the boy was in distress; his main concern was to get him to safety. Besides, the feelings weren't as strong as before. Maybe the boy wasn't as scared, so his feelings weren't as intense.

"Tom spent the next few hours getting the boy to safety and then talking with the police. Afterward he got sick again and ended up in bed for a while. During that time, he was able to think about what had happened. At first he thought he was feeling ill because of all the attention directed at him, but when he was alone, he began to think he had gotten ill because of feeling what the boy had felt when he was lost and scared."

When we had finished our food, the waitress stopped by the table to pick up our plates. (Are waitresses trained to get customers out the door as quickly as possible after they're done eating, even if all the other tables are empty? I've had that impression many times when I've been in restaurants.) The waitress was young and seemed a little nervous putting the check on the table, telling us she would pick it up when we were ready. She could probably see we were involved in a serious conversation and didn't want to interrupt us. Even though both Andrea and I had said we didn't need anything more when she had asked earlier, I ordered a piece of apple pie with ice cream. I said it with one of my charming smiles, and she quickly returned it with a smile of her own, appearing more comfortable, saying it would be no problem. As she prepared to leave the table, she asked if the meal was all right.

"It was fine. Could we each get a cup of coffee also?"

"Sure," she replied as she added the additional items to the check before walking away from the table.

"You're not flirting with the pretty, young help are you, Danny?" Andrea asked as the waitress walked away.

"Oh, you know me. It never hurts to flirt."

This brought out a laugh in Andrea. "As I remember it, you got in a few fights in high school and college for flirting with the wrong girls."

"Yeah, I forgot about that," I said slowly. "But let's get back to what you were saying about Tom. You don't really believe he was hearing the boy's thoughts, do you?"

It was sad to see the smile fade and the brightness that had just shone in Andrea's eyes disappear so quickly, but I knew she would feel better when she had finished telling me about Tom.

"Let's just say that at the time I didn't. Even Tom said he couldn't believe it at first. He knew the idea about finding the boy was real, but he kept telling himself that, logically, it couldn't be. What he kept coming back to though was how he felt inside. That bothered him more than what he thought he heard in his mind.

"When he felt better and all the attention he received on campus began to wane, he went out to see if there was anything to the crazy idea that had entered his mind. Tom, being such an introvert, would avoid crowds if he could, but he went looking for people, especially kids. On a couple of warmer days he went to the park. There was a play at the elementary school in town that he forced himself to go to also. But nothing happened either time. There were no children's voices in his head. He tried the trick they use in movies, looking at a particular kid and concentrating, but all he got was a feeling that someone would think he was weird or a pervert if they saw him staring at kids.

"He really began to think it was all in his head, that it was just a lingering effect of the illness he had experienced earlier in the year.

He had almost put it out of his mind when it happened again. The excitement and interest Tom had created at college had pretty much abated by that time, but someone said something to him about the boy he had saved, so he decided to get away for the weekend. It was close to Christmastime, so he headed into Green Bay to do some shopping at a mall there.

"Everything started out fine, but then he started hearing a voice in his head and feeling sick inside, just as he had that day in the woods. He was feeling nauseous again, but he had to know if what was happening was real. Because he had not had another incident like the one in the woods he had pretty much convinced himself that he had heard the boy just yelling for help that day in the woods, and he had felt sick inside because he knew a little boy was lost. He told himself that he hadn't heard the boy in his head or felt the boy's emotions. But now with the voice he was hearing he set out to see if another child was in trouble.

"As before, he had a good idea about which direction the voice was coming from, so he walked that way. It quickly became apparent to him that this time it definitely was in his head because no one else was reacting to the child's cries—those of a girl, it sounded like to him. The mall was crowded and noisy, but if he could hear the girl, at least one other person should have been able to hear her also. But besides the normal noise and confusion of the mall at that time of year no one seemed to hear what he was hearing.

"Though the words were jumbled like the time in the woods, the impression he was able to get was that the girl was not lost but was being abducted. He followed the voice and the feeling until he saw a little blond-haired girl, maybe four or five years old, being led by a middle-aged man. The girl looked scared and was crying. It wasn't bawling but something more timid. Most people just passed by the pair, oblivious to them. Those who did notice the little girl crying seemed uncomfortable. A few of the women, probably mothers themselves, looked sympathetically at the man. Tom wondered what the man had told the girl to keep her from crying for help.

"Even being close to the girl, Tom still couldn't make out the words he was hearing in his mind, but the feeling was unmistakable; it was fear and confusion. He knew the girl didn't belong to the man, and knowing how our society is he knew the man definitely meant her no good.

"The mall had a central court with four walkways leading out in each direction to the larger retail stores. Tom was just about to enter one of the larger stores when he got a feeling from the girl that brought him to the central court. Just as Tom entered the central court, he caught his first glimpse of the man and little girl as they entered the court from the walkway opposite him. The man with the little girl didn't hesitate but turned down the walkway to his left.

"The words and feelings were still assaulting him, but Tom was sure of one thing: if the man got the little girl out of the mall, she would probably never be seen alive again. So Tom came up with a plan. He looked around to see if he could spot any security guards; when he didn't see any, he started to follow the man and girl. He got a little ahead of them on the opposite side of the walkway but was close enough so the man would notice him. And the man did. The first time it was just as he was glancing at the people around him, but when his eyes passed over Tom, Tom made sure he made eye contact with the man.

"This had the effect Tom wanted; the man slowed a little and kept looking at Tom, who would not avert his eyes. Tom knew he probably looked scared and was probably pale from the feelings he was experiencing in connection with the little girl's plight. Regardless, the man kept looking at Tom, and Tom just stared back. The man had slowed down a little, and Tom advanced a few steps toward them. The man pulled the little girl into one of the small stores they were passing.

"It was a clothing store, and Tom could see the man peering at him over one of the circular racks. Tom couldn't see the little girl, but by the feelings he had he knew the man still had a hold of her hand. There was a salesgirl talking to some customers at a rack at the front of the store, and Tom stepped in front of the customers. The salesgirl started to say she was helping other customers when Tom told her it was an emergency, and she needed to call security. This got the salesgirl's attention, and when Tom pointed to the man and the salesgirl looked in his direction, the man realized his plan would not succeed. The man bolted from the store without the girl."

The waitress continued to pass our table, but she no longer said anything as she stopped and filled our coffee mugs. Andrea didn't pause in her narrative. I don't know how much of Andrea's story the waitress overheard, but she did seem to listen whenever she was near us. I wondered what she thought from the few snippets she was catching.

"Tom again told the salesgirl to call security and give them a description of the fleeing man, so her attention went to the man. Tom walked toward the rack the man had tried to hide behind. Before he got there, he could still feel the fear and confusion radiating from the little girl. When he walked around the rack, he saw the little girl standing there, tears streaming down her face. Tom bent down on one knee and told the little girl she was safe now; the bad man was gone. Maybe it was the way Tom said it or maybe the girl could sense his feelings, as Tom could sense hers, but the girl threw herself into his arms. Tom could then sense a change in her feelings. Her relief was so strong Tom almost threw up right there. He realized that even good feelings could be overpowering.

"The one thing Tom didn't want was to get mixed up with the police or the media again, so he picked the little girl up and took her to the sales counter where the clerk had gone to use a phone. Again, he told the little girl everything was all right and that the salesgirl would help find her parents. He then told the clerk the man had been trying to kidnap the little girl and to watch her until security showed up. When the clerk looked down at the girl, Tom turned and left, not slowing down or looking back when the clerk called out to him."

Andrea paused here and let out a breath, as if telling the story had tired her. I wondered if Andrea was waiting for me to say something or trying to get her thoughts back in order. Even if I wasn't sure if I believed her story, I wanted to know more.

"Did they catch the man?"

"I asked Tom that same question. I'd like to think you and I both want to know because we care about what happened to the little girl and want a child predator to get what he had coming to him, but I can't answer it. Tom said he never tried to find out. For him it was enough to know he had helped the girl. Besides, he ended up sick in bed for almost a week. He was glad he had been able to help the two children, but he couldn't stand having to feel what they did."

"That's quite a story, Andi, but I'm not sure if I believe it. Didn't you say he convinced you? How did he do that?"

"He told me all this about six months after the incident with the little girl. I had not seen much of him over that period of time—I mean, even less than usual, so when I did see him, I asked him what was going on. He told me the story I just told you. And, like you, I questioned it when he was finished. I didn't think he was lying, but I wondered if he could have been wrong about what he thought he heard or felt. I asked him if that could be the case."

"And what did he say?"

"Let's just say he showed me. It was the height of summer, so when he called to say he wanted to see me, I took some vacation time. After he told me his story and I voiced my doubt, he said we were going on a road trip. He was still living in the Upper Peninsula, so we headed to the Lower Peninsula. We went down the coast of Lake Michigan to Ludington because he wanted to be somewhere with a lot of people around. It was a hot Saturday, and though it was quite windy the beach was crowded. He figured if we hung out all day, at least one child had to get separated from his or her parents. He said he found that it happened more often than you would think, but it was usually just a few minutes before the kids and their parents found each other. He was hoping he could find a lost child before the parents did.

"The first few hours were uneventful, and I might have enjoyed myself, catching some sun, if I hadn't seen how uncomfortable Tom appeared to be every time I looked at him. I realized he didn't really want to be there, but he was doing it because I doubted the truth of his story. I actually thought of telling him we should leave, but the sun felt so good, and I really believed the reason we came to the beach would be a bust. I wish I had said something; I wish I had never doubted him.

"Well, it was probably just after two o'clock when I looked over at Tom and noticed he was extremely pale, as if he was going to be sick. I was just about to ask him if he was all right when he said something like "not that" or "why that" or something along those lines. Before I could say anything, Tom got to his feet and started to walk down the beach. I believe he wanted to run to wherever he thought the problem was, but whatever he was feeling was causing him to stagger, as if his equilibrium was messed up. He actually stopped a couple of times and tried to throw up. It was more of a dry heave. Tom probably hadn't eaten or drunk anything because he knew what would happen if he was right. Whatever was going on was scaring me. I think at that moment I started to believe him.

"I tried to ask him what was happening, but I don't think he even heard me. I looked down the beach in the direction he had started to walk to see if there was a kid who looked lost; everything looked normal. But something was definitely wrong with Tom. He kept crying *no!* and *not that!* and trying to hurry along the beach, but he was staggering more than he was walking. He was more of a spectacle than anything else. We had walked maybe twenty yards when Tom dropped down to his hands and knees on the sand and retched again. He seemed to be saying over and over again, "I couldn't help him." One man who had been watching Tom started laughing and said to me, "Had too much to drink, huh?" I just sheepishly grinned to avoid the truth, though I was still unsure what the truth was.

"I was bending over to check on him when Tom looked at me, and the sadness and anguish displayed on his face chilled me. "I can't do this any longer" was all he said, and then a scream from up the beach diverted my attention. It wasn't a scream of fun, and, as bad as I felt for the way Tom looked, I knew something terrible was happening. It took only a second for me to see people pointing out over the lake and someone running into the water. I saw a man diving into one of the advancing waves. He disappeared for about ten or fifteen seconds and then resurfaced, something dangling in his arms. Even though I couldn't see the object that well, I knew what it was before the man was able to stand and walk out of the water. Seeing the lifeless form of the small boy's body was sickening to look at."

Andrea stopped speaking and just stared down at the table in front of her, her hands fidgeting with her now empty coffee cup. We both had refused any more coffee the last time the waitress stopped by the table. She had left us alone after that, walking by silently every now and then to see if I had left money with the bill. I could pretty much guess the rest of Tom's story and was sure Andrea had said about all she wanted to say, but I felt she still needed to finish.

"So what happened then?"

It took a long time for Andrea to answer. For a while, I wondered if she was going to speak, though I wouldn't have blamed her if she hadn't.

"You see, that's the worst part, Danny. He wasn't able to save the boy. Instead, all he could do was feel what the boy felt as he was dying. Tom said there was no way to describe what he felt, and then, with pleading eyes, he asked me to think about it and try to imagine it. I tried and realized quickly I didn't want to. It was probably at that moment when he decided to avoid people as much as possible. That decision deeply changed him.

"I don't know if I can blame him; I saw what experiencing the kid's fear, pain, and confusion did to him. I probably would have made the same decision. But with the decision came the realization that some kids he might be able to help might not get that help from others. The boy might have died in the woods if he hadn't followed the voice. The girl in the mall might have been abused and killed. He was glad he had helped those kids, but he couldn't go back to that place in order to help others. Before, he had never understood what kids felt in situations like that. As he explained to me, why would someone agree to be tortured if they could avoid it? I don't know if he was trying to convince me or himself.

"So he bought himself a house out in the middle of nowhere and basically became a recluse. The nearest town was some twenty miles away and had a population of maybe four hundred people. The computer age was a godsend for Tom. He was quite intelligent and got a job as an information specialist in which he could work from home, writing and editing manuals and presentations for others. He also changed his name at that time. I think he wanted to completely start over in every way possible—to cut all ties to his past.

"But the decision he made bothered him for the rest of his life; he felt guilty about it. I didn't see him much after that. When I did, we were different to each other. I don't think he was happy with himself.

Maybe it had something to do with him dying so young. His decision had to have eaten at him something fierce."

Andrea stopped talking again, and this time I didn't ask her anything else. With silence planted firmly around the table, I just retrieved the money to pay the bill and put it on the check. The waitress must have been keeping an eye on us, for she picked up the bill soon after I placed the money on it. I wondered if the look on either Andrea's face or mine was dour, for though she smiled she didn't say anything as she walked away.

We both silently stood up and left the restaurant. We didn't talk about Tom over the next four days we spent together. With the story told, something had changed in us also. Hopefully we can get past it in the visits we have in the future.

The story about Tom remains in my mind. I can't imagine what he must have gone through. I'm not completely sure everything Andrea told me is true, though I know that she believes it all. Even so, a question haunts me. If it was all true and I had been in Tom's place, would I have made the same decision?

Baggage

Some people are natural-born storytellers. They have what some call the gift of gab. It doesn't matter if the story is one of fact or fiction; once they start telling their story, you just want them to continue talking. When I was growing up, I had a neighbor who was one of those storytellers. He told all the kids in the neighborhood many stories over the years. This was a time before there were DVDs and video games and any of the other types of distractions children have nowadays. During the summer, we would play outside all day, and then, in the evening, we would gather either on his porch or around the fire pit in his backyard, if he had a fire going, to listen to one of his stories. Over the years, I heard hundreds of stories. I've forgotten many of them over time, but there is still one I remember well. It wasn't a story I heard as a kid but one I heard from him when I was a young adult.

I'm much older now. I don't have the ability to tell stories like my neighbor did, but it doesn't mean I shouldn't tell the story myself. I believe it is more important that this story *is* told than *how* it is told. I'm an old man now, and I've had a full life. As with any life lived, there are a few regrets, a few unfulfilled dreams, but overall I can't complain. I've had the good along with the bad. And there have been times when good luck has smiled down on me. And that's really what this story is all about: good and bad luck and accepting whatever comes our way.

During the high point of the summer for the past ten years or so, my wife, Lydia, and I have hosted a family reunion on our property. The other two family reunions we try to go to each year have an attendance of upwards of a hundred people and have been a yearly event for ninety years on my side of the family and eighty years on my wife's side. Our reunion consists of just Lydia and me, our six children, and their families. I believe our children decided to initiate this more intimate reunion as another way, besides Christmas, for our whole immediate family to be together. With our family spread far and wide across the country, only about half of the immediate family could make it to one or the other of the larger family reunions. But for the last ten years, my wife and I have been blessed to have everyone together for at least three days, with some of them staying as long as a week.

The second day of our reunion is what we refer to as "the event day." There are no side trips for any of our kids or grandchildren. The furthest anyone might venture from the property is a bicycle ride along some roads around the area. The horseshoes, volleyball, and other yard games are in use, and the grills are full of a variety of meats, while the picnic tables are full of side dishes, salads, and desserts.

As this particular event day began to wane into evening, the adults had all retired to lawn chairs situated around the fire pit, which our eldest son, Bill, was filling with kindling and firewood. It wouldn't be long before the evening bonfire would be roaring. Most of the grandchildren were still playing games in the yard, but Bill's two oldest, Taryn and Josh, were sitting on one of the logs that circled the fire pit. All three logs would be filled with the other kids once the fire was blazing and the cool evening air began to set in. Taryn and Josh were involved in a conversation between themselves, but as their voices were raised a little with excitement, most of the adults were soon listening to them. Taryn had gone for a bike ride that morning with her cousin, Beth, and was telling Josh about an old abandoned house they had passed.

"It can't compare to the old house that your grandpa there used to live near when he was a boy," my second oldest son, Tom, interjected when there was a momentary pause from the children.

"That house was downright creepy," Bill added with a hint of nostalgia in his voice.

The young kids looked at Bill when he said *creepy,* and then everyone looked toward me because the house Bill spoke of was near the house I had grown up in as a child. I had spent the first eighteen years of my life there and had continued to visit the place until my father died, and my mother went to live with my sister. It had been many years since I had been to that house. Unlike most people who think from time to time of the home they lived in as a child, the house I thought of most from my childhood was not my own but that creepy house down the road.

"There is quite a story that goes along with that house," I said to an attentive audience.

"Was it haunted?" Josh asked in a low voice tinged with a hint of excitement and fear.

Tom quickly added that his son, Josh, was like most boys his age and showed interest in the spooky and macabre. I wondered for a minute if I told him the story that was on my mind, it might be unhealthy for his imagination. But then again, the story wasn't really scary.

"Oh no, nothing scary," I chuckled. I noticed the look Bill and Tom exchanged and wondered what stories they had heard about the house when they were children, when Lydia and I had taken them to see their grandparents. Some of them were probably the same stories I had heard when I was a boy, though they were very far from reality. I had held the true story inside for many years. Now, with all eyes upon me, I was glad at last to share what I knew. It was a story that needed to be told. "But it doesn't mean the story isn't interesting," I added.

Because I knew the other kids would want to hear the story, I told Taryn and Josh to round up the others before I began. The two of them quickly scampered off, and in less than fifteen minutes everyone was gathered around the roaring fire.

"Well, tell us already," Tom voiced what I could see in everyone's eyes, including my wife's. So with a wry smile and quick wink, I settled back to tell the story. I only wished I could tell it as well as it had been told to me.

"You little ones don't know the house I'm talking about, but your grandmother and your parents do, especially Bill and Tom, as they're the oldest and probably remember the house quite well."

I paused for a moment until the eyes that had glanced toward Bill and Tom returned to me, and then I prepared to continue. It gave me a twinge of satisfaction to see the children of Bill and Tom looking at their dads with something akin to awe, hearing that they were a part of the story. Even though the young ones seemed the most excited, I could tell that my kids and their spouses were ready to hear the story also.

"Anyone who's ever grown up in the country knew a house like the one I'm talking about. As far back as I can remember, that house—the Haller house—was a worn-down, dilapidated shack of a building. It would have been the perfect setting for a haunted house or ghost story. I mean, every time I see the Norman Bates house in *Psycho,* I think of the Haller house from my childhood. And, believe me, all the kids I knew believed the house was haunted. The Haller house wasn't the only old, run-down house around, but there was something different about the place, and some of it had to do with the fact that there was someone living there. We would sneak around the other buildings, dare each other to venture inside, but beyond looking at the Haller house from the road, I don't recall any of the kids ever stepping onto the property.

"We had all heard how someone was living in the house, and I do seem to remember seeing lights streaming from the windows a couple of times. But as the house sat back from the road a ways and the brush had grown up around the property, you really wouldn't notice the house from the road unless you were looking for it. And when we did see lights in the house, it just reinforced our notion that ghosts were playing tricks.

"As I've said, there were other creepy-looking houses in the area, so we focused our attention on those houses. We talked and whispered about the other haunted houses, but deep down, the house we were scared of—the one we wouldn't even talk about—was the Haller house.

"Eventually we grew up, and other things became more important to us. I had not given much thought to the house until summer break of my first year in college. It was an early Friday evening, and I was sitting out in the back yard with my mother, sister, and our neighbor, Sam, who was a good friend of the family. My father was standing over the grill near us, and he and Sam were talking. I had been home for a little less than a week, and my mom was filling me in on all the local news. I was listening to her in an offhand way, though I hoped it appeared that I was being attentive to her while listening to my father and Sam to find out if their conversation was more interesting. When Sissy came back from the house with some refreshments, she must have noticed that I wasn't really into our mother's conversation, for she patted me on the shoulder and got mother involved in a conversation that was more suited to the two of them.

"I had just about tuned everything out when I realized Sam and my father were talking about how demolition of the Haller house was to begin in about a week. My interest was instantly piqued. The mention of that house stirred many emotions and memories in me, even after so many years. My mother then explained that she had forgotten Mr. Haller's death was some of the news she wanted to tell my sister and me. (My mother was one of those who could be having an in-depth conversation with someone but was still capable of knowing the topics of all the other conversations around her.)

"'You mean someone really lived there?' I asked with keen interest. That had been the rumor the whole time I was a kid, but I wasn't sure I actually believed it.

"'Yes. It wasn't haunted like you all thought when you were kids,' my mother began, and I know she would have continued if my dad hadn't interjected.

"'You knew Mr. Haller pretty well, didn't you, Sam?' I'm sure my father knew the answer to that question, but it was his way of politely steering the conversation away from my mother. Bless her soul, but she could prattle on when she got started.

"'I knew John as well as anyone, I suppose. He was a unique person. He was my friend.'

"I was intrigued by the statement. Sam had been almost like one of the family. Besides the stories he told to Sis, our friends, and me, he always had sodas and popsicles for us, and we spent many days playing in his yard. Though I can remember some of his stories—and some were pretty good ghost stories—I don't recall him ever saying anything about the Haller place. As kids we never really talked about it around him, but he must have known how we felt about the place. So there must have been a reason Sam never spoke of Mr. Haller because Sam loved to tell stories. This is the story Sam told us that day.

"'The story of John Haller started long before he moved into that house and became the recluse I knew him as. In fact, it is that little-known story of his early life that directly led to what he eventually became. For the first five years of his life, he was just like most other boys—nothing out of the ordinary. He lived with his family in a tenement in New York City. Like millions of others, they were a part of the lower middle class. One day when John was five, he went outside to play after a rainstorm had moved through the city. There had been some construction going on near his tenement, and, as he passed near the work area, he slipped in the mud and fell into a deep construction hole that had filled with rain water and mud. John had never learned to swim, but luckily there was a construction worker nearby who jumped into the water hole, grabbed John, and handed him safely to another worker.

"'You can talk all you want about coincidences and fate or what you will, but the worker who saved John had some kind of trouble—maybe a cramp or a heart attack. John was never sure what it was, but the worker died before he too could be pulled from the hole. Everybody commented on how lucky John was. What if the worker hadn't been nearby or had experienced his own problem before he could save John? John was thankful that he was saved, but later, when he was a little older, he realized that if the guy hadn't jumped into the hole to save him he wouldn't have died. I can't imagine how that situation would play on the mind of a child, but I think it could be quite the baggage to carry around.

"'John may not have continued to view things the same way later in life, but that early incident was only the beginning. A few years later, he was on a bus with his mother, and the bus was involved in an accident. The shock of the bus hitting another vehicle caused a stranger to fall into John, knocking John out of the way just as a piece of metal flew through the bus and impaled the stranger in the same spot where John had been moments before. For the second time, John could have died but was spared at the expense of another.

"'An incident like that happening once in a lifetime would be unfortunate. He had punched his golden ticket and lived. But it didn't happen just once or even twice. In fact, John punched his golden ticket on an average of once every two-to-three years from the time he was seven until he was twenty-two. It seemed that, with John, everything came with a price. I suppose John could have said the hell with it and been satisfied with the good fortune that came his way. I'm sure there are many people who would have, but he wasn't able to block out of his mind the misfortune that befell others. After he survived the bus accident, John began to believe he caused the man's death by being the one who survived. He even began to view the earlier construction accident the same way. John didn't think of himself as a pessimistic person, but he could only take so much bad misfortune. He wished he could be happy about his good fortune, and he *was* thankful, but there is a difference between being thankful for something and being happy about it. With John, the price was just too high for him to be happy.

"'It was then, at age twenty-two, that he bought that house and became a recluse. He was able to buy the house because his "luck" also extended to money matters. But even with any material good fortune, there still seemed to be a price to pay. One time, when he was in his late teens, he found a bag with a lot of money in it—thousands of dollars, actually. Like some youths would have done, he looked around; when he didn't see anyone, he pocketed the money. A couple of months later, he read about a man who committed suicide because of financial ruin as a result of losing money he had borrowed from his father-in-law to pay his mortgage. Of course John didn't have proof the money he found belonged to that man. But with the way his luck worked, John figured it had to have been his. He would gladly have given the money back or at least what he hadn't spent, which was most of it, but by then it was too late. The man was dead. John already blamed himself; he didn't need others pointing fingers at him.

"'The only solution John could think of was to distance himself from the rest of the world, so he wouldn't be a curse to others. By moving out in the country and hiding himself away he wouldn't have contact with the outside world. And one thing that worked in his favor by becoming a hermit was that his house, on the exterior at least, became dilapidated-looking. It took about ten years for the house and land to get the look that caused the kids to say the place was haunted. By that time, none of the kids growing up had been there when John moved in, so they had never seen him. It was easy for the rumors to start.

"'When I moved next door to John, I heard some of the stories about him. I heard he was grossly deformed or was a mean-spirited recluse who would just as soon shoot you as yell at you if you stepped onto his property. I was to find out how untrue the rumors were. For the first few months, I saw no activity coming from his house. If I had been like some neighbors, concerned with just myself, I may never have met John. But I'm more outgoing, and I just couldn't stay away. And then part of what drove me to meet him might have been brought on by curiosity. I wanted to know if there was any truth to the rumors. After those first few months, I made my way to his house; with a little trepidation I knocked on his door. He didn't answer at first. In fact, I was ready to think no one was home when I finally heard a faint noise coming from within, so I knocked again. In all, I had to knock four times before the door opened a crack, and I got my first glimpse of the occupant inside.

"'My first thought, brought on by the stories the kids all whispered, was that John didn't look like a monster. Even as adults it's amazing how the words of others can dictate our ideas and opinions. There is no reason why I should have thought he would be any different from me, and I suppose, deep down inside, I knew he would be just like me. But for a few seconds I let my imagination get the better of me.

"'I explained to him that I was his neighbor and wanted to introduce myself. It appeared at first that John either didn't understand what I was saying or didn't want to be in my company, but slowly his demeanor changed. You could see the stress in his face relax. Now that I know his whole story and I reflect back on that day, I think he had been so lonely for so long that he was actually a little relieved when someone reached out to him. He invited me in.

"As I stepped into his house, I was overwhelmed by the world I entered. One would never think the inside of the house would be in the condition it was by the look of the outside. The inside of the house was immaculate. It was homey, and I instantly felt at ease. The other thing I noticed was the inordinate number of books in the house. In every room I walked into, including the foyer, the walls were lined with bookcases. As I got to know John better and saw more of his house, that observation remained true. Even the bathroom and kitchen had a couple of small bookshelves in them.

"'The conversation I had with John that first day consisted mainly of introductions. He was quite cordial with me, but there was no invitation to return when I left. I didn't, however, get the impression that he felt my visit had been an intrusion. I couldn't figure out exactly what feeling I was getting from John, but I sensed I would not be turned away if I visited him again. There was also something quite mysterious about him, so I knew I would visit him in the future. As I continued to spend time with him, he opened up more and more; gradually he told me his story. It became obvious that John was a very intelligent yet sympathetic person. I was glad when the guarded loneliness I had witnessed the first day I met him began to fade.

"'As he told me more of his story, I was filled with mixed feelings. There was no way I could ever fully comprehend the guilt he spoke of. He told me about a time when he was sixteen, and his father and uncle took him deer hunting. He was in the woods with his uncle, working on a blind for John to hunt from. His uncle was bent over when the sound of a gunshot rang out close by. Just as his uncle stood up and looked in the direction of the sound, another shot echoed through the woods. A bullet entered his uncle's body, lodging in his spine and killing him instantly. If his uncle had not stood up, the bullet would have passed over his head and struck John instead.

"'After being spared several times already, how do you reconcile yourself to the fact that you are spared again at the expense of a family member? How can you be thankful? It's one thing to be spared by someone you don't know—even this carries with it guilt—but how are you supposed to feel when it is someone you know and care about? How can the guilt not become unbearable?

"'The other emotion I felt was one of thankfulness—not because I wasn't facing something as terrible as what John had faced but just grateful for the life I had lived, as simple as it had been. You could hear in John's voice how sad and lonely he was. Even though he was knowledgeable about the world around him from the reading he did, he was missing out on actual experiences. He figured if he remained a recluse, no one else would get hurt. And with all the painful memories of his youth, he could not remember walking along a beach or a dusty road at sunset. He could not remember what it was like to look up at the stars at night. He had allowed the trees to encroach around his house so much that he wouldn't have had a good view of the night sky if he tried to look up from his porch. And because he could not remember events like that, all of a sudden I appreciated those simple, everyday occurrences.

"'We continued our friendship over the years, and I was able to help him in many ways. Before we met, John had paid the man in town who owned the general store extra money to deliver supplies late in the evening once a week. I took over that chore for John, though I wished at times he would get out and do it himself or even travel into town with me. When I told him what some of the rumors were concerning him, he conceded he was both pleased and saddened. He was pleased in the sense that maybe it would keep people away but saddened by the fact that he had to live in such a solitary manner.

"'Even with all the information John conveyed to me, I was still surprised when he told me he had not been out of his house in over ten years. I began to hound him to go outside. I tried to explain that the chances of something happening during a walk along the road or a trip into town were very slim. But as John said, the chance was still there. He believed the chance was greatly increased because of who he was. And truthfully, he didn't know if his nerves could handle being around other people. In fact, he was on pins and needles every time I visited him. He could envision a scenario where he slipped and started to fall. Instinctively I might reach to help him and, in the process, might slip myself, hitting my head or falling down and breaking my neck. For me, it was a remote possibility, but for John it wasn't a matter of whether or not it could happen but when.

"'One thing that did happen, which I was thankful for, was that I was eventually able to talk John into sitting outside with me at the back of his house to enjoy the outdoors. Of course he would only do it late at night; he didn't want to risk the chance of anyone else seeing him. But I didn't care once I saw the pleasure on his face as he looked up at the few stars we could see, a cool breeze washing over both of us. Even then you could still tell he was troubled inside by that guilt about those who had died or suffered in one way or another.

"'I was never able to work John back into society. The wounds that had scarred him over the years were just too many and too deep. Sometimes the baggage we carry will weigh us down for the rest of our lives. I guess for years I had romanticized the situation; I imagined that before John died his life would somehow be redeemed by saving the life of someone else. But life rarely proceeds the way we feel it should, the way we read in novels or see in movies. Eventually John died; it was a quiet ending to a life that started so eventfully. I also believe John died sooner than he should have. It was almost as if he had given up on life. Maybe the guilt he carried was finally too much for him to bear.'"

My audience was quiet as I finished telling the story I had heard those many years before. I could only imagine what they were thinking, but I hoped it was akin to what I had felt since I first heard the story: even when things were going bad in my life or something was getting me down, I would remember the life of John. Even though his life was sad, it could be a lesson to us. We all could use a little inspiration from time to time.

Haunted

In the memories of my childhood I can still hear the voices of my parents assuring me that there were no monsters under my bed or in my closet. They tried to explain to me that the darkness was just an absence of light and not a breeding ground for things that wanted to tear the flesh from my bones or rip me open and eat my insides. As a young boy, I often cowered under my blankets, breathing rapidly until the air became stale. I would shake with fear even though I believed wholeheartedly that the monsters couldn't get me as long as no part of my body was exposed to the darkness beyond my covers.

I've heard this phenomenon is common among young children. Maybe those fears and the belief that one is safe under a blanket is the origin of the "security blanket" that so many children have trouble letting go of. Maybe we all look to something to get us through those years of fear: a blanket, a nightlight, sleeping with our parents, or having them stay with us until we fall asleep. We do what we have to until we get old enough to learn that the monsters aren't real—at least not those monsters.

Though the memories have never left me, they've become more vivid recently as my son is now going through his own stage of night terrors. I try to assure him that there are no monsters in the dark, just as my parents had tried to assure me. And as far as the creatures that haunt a child's darkness, I know they're not real. But there are real monsters in the world, and there are real reasons to be scared.

When my son gets older, I will explain to him the truth that has haunted me since the summer I turned fourteen. I will explain to him how he needs to watch over and protect his little sister. She isn't quite two years old, but the little ones grow up so fast. My son must be prepared as early as possible and know the importance of his task. If only I had known the importance of that task sooner. But no matter how hard I wanted to change the memories, the facts remained the same.

I still dream about the summer when my sister, Katie, was taken. But unlike my memories, the dreams deviate from the facts. Sometimes in my dreams I see her taken. I see her harmed, and I hear her scream. The scream is penetrating, fearful, and pained. And it is always the same three words she is screaming out: *Help me, Georgie!* I can't see who is hurting her because it is only a shadow. I see and hear all this, and, as much as I would like to help her (my God, I wish I could help her), I am never able to. Other times in my dreams she is just lost to me; I can't hear her being hurt, but even those dreams tear at me.

After all these years, I still wake up more often than I like with a scream on my lips, my body trembling and covered in sweat. For some reason I can't tell my wife the truth about the terror that grips my heart, so I maintain the façade she has always known, that I can't remember the specifics of the dreams that gives me night chills so bad. But I was honest with her when I told her I became a writer as a way of dealing with my nightmares.

As a writer of horror novels and stories, I've spent a career scaring people. I've written about ghosts, aliens, vampires, werewolves, crazed killers, possessed people, and demons. There are other tricks I've used, but they can all be grouped together by what kids would describe as "monsters." People have a predilection for adrenalin rushes, and fear can be a powerful motivator. Whether it's a book they read or a movie they see or an event they witness or participate in people like to be scared. Why do you think haunted houses and rollercoasters are so popular?

But it's a false fear that people are comfortable with. It's a fear they can get away from by putting down the book or shutting off the movie. It's okay to be scared, as long as what they believe is scaring them is not real. Maybe that is a way for people to deal with the real fears that hide deep within themselves. My therapist says I write horror stories as a way to deal with my own fears.

I was fortunate that my first novel was a bestseller, regardless of it being so rudimentary. It put me in demand for lectures, seminars, and book signings. I used those events for my own benefit, garnering many ideas for future writing. And at the book signings people loved to tell me what really scared them. I used many pseudonyms for different forms of stories to see if I could sell my work for what it was and not for my name. But no matter how many different genres of writing I tried it seems I always returned to what was the easiest for me to write, what came naturally. As I became rich and famous for writing horror stories, it eventually became my exclusive genre.

Sometimes there's no satisfaction in being heralded for the talent one has. There's no joy in winning awards or being considered a legend in one's own field. As I said, people like to be scared, and I pour as much fear into my stories as I can. But I am not like most people. I hate being scared. Instead of getting an adrenalin rush through my veins, sweat breaks out on my brow and palms. Fear to me is real. I try to relieve my fear—exorcise it from my soul—by pouring it on paper. Most of the time, I'm not even sure what I'm writing about until I finish and go back to edit it. Somehow I bring a story from the deep, dark recesses of my mind while all I'm thinking of is the one memory that has haunted me since that summer so long ago.

In spite of bringing so much fear and pain to my life the memory has a bright beginning. It was one of those warm, lazy, sunny summer days that people like to talk about nostalgically. Even though there are still days like it every summer, people enjoy reminiscing about them as if they're a thing of the past.

I had spent the day playing outside, back when children wanted to be outside and were upset when it rained. But even then, they didn't have trouble going outside and getting wet. Building dams on a dirt road to see how much water could be backed up was one of my favorite activities. It was a time before video games and computers, a time when imagination was a child's greatest asset.

Tommy, my best friend, had gone with his parents to visit his Aunt Martha. So instead of playing on the many trails we had forged along the river in the woods behind our houses, I spent most of the day in the tree house we had built. It wasn't really much of a tree house, just a haphazard shamble of leftover boards our fathers had given us when they had finished one of their projects. I'm not sure if our fathers planned it to their advantage or were just happy to spend the time with us, but both Tommy and I would willingly help when one of our dads was building something. They were so glad for our help that we would get a couple of good boards along with the leftover pieces. Though our tree house wasn't much to look at, I think we did a pretty good job with what we had to work with.

I had just finished some of the improvements Tommy and I had discussed the last time we had been together in the tree house when my mother called for me. I hadn't noticed that the sun had started its downward journey for the day. My mother called out for the third time—the maximum number she allowed before I got in trouble for not answering—before I put the tree house in order for the night, swung down the branches to the ground, and bounded across the backyard to the door where my mother stood waiting for me. She waited until I reached the screen door and stood there, with my full attention on her, before she spoke again.

"I'm starting to get supper ready, so I need you to go to the park and get your sister. And don't dawdle, or your supper will get cold."

After lunch, Katie had gone to the town's only park to play with some of her friends. The park wasn't that large, but it did have a slide, some swings, and a few of those spring animals to play on. Tommy and I would go to the park occasionally, but there wasn't enough there to keep our interest for long. So even on the days when we did visit the park, it wasn't long before we found ourselves back on our trails or along the stream or in our tree house. There was a cement slab on which the girls could jump rope or play hopscotch. But Tommy and I joked with each other (though I firmly believed it) that the girls could play in the park as long as they did because their imaginations were inferior to ours.

I made an about-face and headed for the woods that bordered the back of our yard. My mother didn't say anything. Even though Katie had walked down the road to the park—and that's the route Mother would have taken had she gone to get Katie—she knew it was quicker for me to take one of my trails. Tommy and I had made trails that could get us to pretty much any place in town the woods were near. As I started along one of the trails, I realized how hungry I was. So, in spite of my mother's statement, I had my own reason for not dawdling.

I made it to the park in about half the time it would have taken along the road. Katie was with her friends; she was bent over, drawing something in chalk on the cement slab. The slab was situated near the entrance to the park from the road, so Katie hadn't noticed me arriving at the park. I had just started to walk toward Katie when I noticed

Sherry Lohman sitting on one of the few benches in the park. It wasn't until I got older that I realized what I felt toward Sherry that summer was just a boyhood crush. But at the time, I thought I was in love with her. I got excited around her and could actually feel my heart rate quicken in my chest whenever I saw her. When I first started having these feelings for Sherry, I would have trouble finding words to say or stammer out the ones I did attempt when I tried to talk to her. I had gotten somewhat better since those first few awkward encounters.

I became more comfortable around Sherry when it became obvious that she liked me also, at least a little. I didn't think it was possible for anyone to have such strong feelings as I had. But she talked to me when I tried to converse with her. I believe the softness in her voice came more from shyness than not wanting to talk to me. Then some of the other girls in our class, her friends, told me that Sherry *did* like me. After that it was so much easier to talk to her.

I hadn't seen much of her since the school year ended the previous month. I may have been entering a phase where girls were becoming something more than creatures who were a nuisance, but I was still a young boy who thrived in his imaginary world. So I continued to spend most of my time playing with Tommy.

It had been a couple of weeks since I had seen Sherry, so the rush of excitement I felt was greater than it had been for some time. She was reading a book and didn't notice me; for a second I wondered how I would get her attention without being obvious or making the situation awkward. I could think of only one course of action to take. I would walk over and get Katie, acting as though I hadn't noticed Sherry, and I would wait until the way back when I was almost to the trail before I took notice of her. I would ask Katie about her day—small talk—so it would seem believable that I hadn't noticed Sherry. That way I would leave it to her to make the first move—at least I hoped she would. That was my plan.

My mind was aflutter as I walked toward Katie. If Sherry said she liked to come to the park to read, and did with any frequency, I could find myself visiting the park more often. I was already trying to figure out excuses to give to Tommy so that I could come to the park. He knew how I felt about Sherry but still believed that girls were a foreign or alien entity and to be avoided if possible. I couldn't wait for the female bug to hit Tommy, so I could tease him about it the way he teased me. But deep inside I knew that would bring to an end a certain phase of the friendship Tommy and I shared.

As I neared the cement slab where Katie and her friends were playing, I yelled out to her. When she looked over at me, I told her it was time to go home for supper. After some quick good-byes to her friends, she picked up her jump rope and bounded along beside me as I started to walk back toward the trail. I didn't want to make it obvious that I knew Sherry was in the park, so I kept my head turned toward Katie as we walked, asking her how her day had been and what she had done. We were almost to the bench when I heard Sherry's voice.

"Hi, George. Hi, Katie."

I looked over to the bench; she had said hi to both of us, but Sherry was looking at me. I was greeted with her crystal-blue eyes and the smile I found cute despite the one side tooth that jutted out ever so slightly. It wasn't noticeable when she talked, but there it was every time she smiled.

"Oh, hi, Sherry. I didn't see you there." I felt a little guilty when I said that because I knew it wasn't true. For a second I wondered if she knew I was lying; I didn't want to look in her eyes any longer, so I looked at Katie. "Our mom sent me here to get Katie for supper."

Though I was much more comfortable now around Sherry, I was still a little nervous. I'm sure it showed as I started to ramble on with my conversation. "Do you come here often to read?" Now I did look back at Sherry. "Maybe I'll see you here another time. I don't see you that often now that school is out for the summer."

When I looked back over to Sherry, she was smiling at Katie. When I stopped talking, she looked back at me. That slight nervous flutter intensified throughout my body. First crushes can be so confusing.

"Yeah, I like coming here when the weather is nice. Maybe we could see each other here some time, when you could stay for a while."

It was at that point that Katie reached out and tugged on my hand. It was a tug that would forever stick in my memory and one that pulled at more than just my hand whenever I thought back on it.

"Come on, Georgie, let's go home."

I can only think now that Katie must have been hungry because she had always been friendly with Sherry before. She would actually beam whenever she saw Sherry. And there couldn't be any jealousy. Katie had never shown it before, and she knew she was my little angel.

"In a minute." I've tried to remember if there was any anger or snappiness in my voice. I would like to think there wasn't, but maybe that is my way of trying to alleviate the guilt that has been my constant companion since the events of that day. Even if there had been some unwarranted tone in my voice, it was not from my heart, of that I am sure. But my mind was preoccupied with Sherry, so I can't recall how my voice sounded. As my eyes darted between Sherry's face and her jutting tooth, I didn't see what kind of reaction was on Katie's face.

As happens with anyone who dwells on an unforgettable and regrettable incident in the past, I can only speculate how things might have been if just one thing had happened differently that day. What if I had not taken the trail to the park but the road instead? Then I would have come upon Katie on the other side of the park and may never have noticed Sherry. What if I hadn't been drawn to that tooth of Sherry's that jutted outward ever so slightly and held my attention so raptly? After that day, the tooth was no longer cute or attractive to me but seemed to jut toward me accusingly, pointing at me specifically no matter which side of Sherry I stood on.

And what if I hadn't let Katie's hand slip from mine? Of the many what-ifs in my mind over the years, that is the one that has affected me the most. I could have held on tighter or let her pull me along with her; either way she would have stayed with me. But instead, I let go of her hand. Of all the images, dreams, and nightmares I've had since, the one that has haunted me the most by far involves our hands. The dreams have taken many forms even though the message has always been the same: I let Katie slip away. I let go of her hand.

One image I have is of Katie and me standing on the corner of a busy intersection, and her hand slips from mine as she steps out into the street. I never really see her face or body; my attention is focused on our hands and the space that begins to grow between them. Though I've had this dream repeatedly, each time is like the first. I'm not really alarmed by what is happening until I hear a screech of tires, and Katie yelling for me. I always wake up just as I start to yell for her; sometimes her name echoes in the darkness as I am jolted from my dream. Other times my call to her remains in my dream, fading slowly away.

Another common dream I have is where Katie and I are in the middle of the ocean with no land in sight. I am sitting in a life raft with my arm over the side. I am holding Katie's hand as she is in the water by the side of the raft. I am the only one in the raft, which is quite large, but for some reason I don't try to pull Katie out of the water or even ask if she would like to be in the raft with me. We both seem to be content with the situation we're in. As in many dreams, aspects that aren't completely logical when awake seem to be nothing out of the ordinary in the dream. Most dreams seem to have their own logic.

Again, Katie's hand slowly and gently slips away from mine. All is well, and I'm completely at ease with the situation until I hear Katie's voice calling out my name. I look down at the water and see her hand ready to disappear into the depths of the ocean while her voice still pleads for me. The logic of real life doesn't invade the dream world, so I don't wonder how she could be calling to me from under the water. I just hear the urgency of her cry. There doesn't seem to be any need to hurry on my part as I slowly reach for her hand. But before I can connect with it, her hand vanishes into the void of the water. Katie yells out my name one more time, and it is then that I always wake up.

Returning to that summer of my youth, Katie's hand slipped from mine. It seems that a part of my mind recalls Katie saying something more and that I replied to her, but those words have since been lost. After a few more minutes of talking to Sherry, we both agreed, in a roundabout, childish, shy way, to meet in the park the following day. As I looked to my side, I noticed Katie was not there. Had she said she was going to start back without me? Had I told her to go ahead?

In a recessed corner of my mind I could hear my mother's voice admonishing me to always keep an eye on Katie when we were in the woods, so she wouldn't fall and hurt herself or wander off and get lost. I always tried to comply with my mother's wishes—even if I thought both requests were somewhat foolish. Katie could fall down and get hurt anywhere, and it would be hard for anyone to get lost as long as they stayed on the trails Tommy and I had made. I had told Katie many times to always stay on the trails. So maybe the warnings didn't play as important a part in my mind as they should have. If they had, I surely would have kept a better eye on Katie.

I wasn't overly concerned as I headed toward the trailhead. With a final backward glance and a smile I turned the first corner of the path, and Sherry disappeared from my view, obscured by the thicket of the woods. Only then did I quicken my pace. I still wasn't worried about Katie; I just wanted to catch up to her before we reached our house. That way Mother wouldn't know I had let Katie out of my sight. When I caught up to Katie, I would ask her not to mention to our mother how I had let her slip out of my sight for a few minutes. What Mother didn't know couldn't hurt me.

But I didn't catch up to her. Maybe Katie had said something about being hungry, so she hurried home ahead of me. When I emerged from the woods into the backyard, I was already formulating in my mind what I was going to say to our mother when I entered the house to see Katie already there. I realized the best course of action was to be honest. My mother liked Sherry and knew how I felt about her, and though my mother never said so, I had the impression she thought it was nice that Sherry was my first crush.

I was still feeling care free as I entered through the back door of the house. There was a clear view into the dining room as I walked down the short hallway to the laundry room where I could wash my hands. My mother was putting a steaming bowl of mashed potatoes on the table, and she looked first at me and then behind me as I passed. Then her eyes returned to mine with a quizzical look on her face. And with that look I realized Katie had not made it home yet. I didn't see her in the dining room or hear her in the wash room. Normally my first thought would have been that she was upstairs in her room, but the look in my mother's eyes squashed any possibility of that.

"Isn't Katie with you?"

Over time the ramifications of that one question took on many meanings to me. I'm not sure if my mother meant all of them, but she should have. The question I knew she meant was the obvious one: where was Katie? The other meaning that crept into my soul as time passed was that Katie had been my responsibility. The weight of responsibility can become very heavy over the years if not handled correctly and even more so if it's justified.

The answer I had to give was the same as I had planned, but I hesitated before giving it. In that slight hesitation I saw the uncertainty in my mother's eyes joined by a hint of fear. I stammered out my explanation. It was becoming difficult to say exactly what I wanted to as I saw a rigidness pass through my mother's body. And mentioning Sherry did not have the effect I had hoped for. I'm not sure how much sense my words were making by the time I finished speaking. My mother was looking intently at me as I spoke. I didn't see anger on her face, but it appeared she was trying to think things through in her mind. Figuring her reaction would have been one of anger, I was confused by the lack of it. That just magnified the fear I was beginning to feel. I stood there wondering what I should do.

"Okay, George," my mother finally said after what seemed like an eternity of silence. "I want you to go and sit on the back steps and keep an eye out for Katie."

"I can walk the trail and call for her."

"No, just do as I say. I don't need both of you getting lost."

For a moment I thought of telling her there was no way I could get lost on the trails that Tommy and I had spent so much time making, but I thought better of it. There had been a snap in my mother's voice when she responded to my last statement. Again, I didn't hear anger in her voice, just the tone of finality she used when she wanted action to her requests and not backtalk.

As I pushed through the screen door, I could hear my mother pick up the telephone receiver and start dialing a number. I couldn't quite make out what my mother was saying as she began to talk into the phone. I'm not sure if it was because she was trying to keep her voice low or because the sounds of the outside were louder now that I was in the backyard. And maybe it was because I was trying to decide exactly what I was going to say to Katie when she finally showed up. I wasn't really mad at her and didn't want to admonish her. Mother hadn't yelled at me after all, but she needed to know that she had to mind me when we were together. Maybe if I told her how concerned and scared I had been for her, she would know I was serious.

Activity around the house increased as late afternoon turned into early evening. Cars came and went, including a couple of police vehicles. Some people headed into the woods on the trails—my trails—as I continued to sit on the back steps. Some of the men acknowledged me with a nod as they passed by, but no words were exchanged. It was as if a dome of silence surrounded me. Even my father came home earlier than usual. He had to have left work early. I only saw him off to the side of the house, talking to the police, so he didn't have time to say anything to me. He acknowledged me with his eyes, and I don't remember any anger being there, only concern.

Just as the sun was giving off its final glow over the trees of the woods, my mother appeared at the back door and told me to go to bed. Most nights my mother would wait for me to fire back my complaints, especially if it was early like it was today. But she just turned and went back inside to wait with the other ladies who had come to the house earlier in the evening.

I wasn't in any mood to argue with her anyway. To go to my room would be an escape. With all the activity and still no Katie, my concern now had turned to fear. I was sure something was wrong. And I guess I felt guilt about the situation we faced. Though no one had given me any accusatory looks, there had been some looks of pity. It still didn't change how I felt. I had let my family down, but worse, I had let Katie down. After I had gotten ready and climbed into bed, it seemed I lay there for a very long time listening to the sounds in and around the house, waiting and hoping for some kind of promising news before I fell asleep.

As soon as I awoke the next morning, an ominous feeling was in the air. There were still sounds in the house, but it felt different. I dressed quickly and descended the stairs. When I got to the bottom step and glanced into the living room, my heart sank. As much as I didn't want to believe it, I knew the outcome of the incident. My mother was sitting on the couch, dabbing a handkerchief to her eyes, while my Aunt Bertie had one arm around her back and her other hand on my mother's free arm that rested in her lap. They were gently rocking back and forth while other women my mother knew—some of them I knew only by appearance—were crowded into the room. They were sitting on the available furniture or just standing, looking at my mother and Aunt Bertie with dismay on their faces.

My father was nowhere in sight, but I did notice my Uncle Ken standing in the shadows of one corner of the room. Though the day was already bright, it was almost as if the sun didn't want to shine into the house. Or maybe the pain in the room was keeping the sunlight at bay. What I probably hadn't noticed as a kid was that the blinds weren't open all the way. We so often want to attribute to the dark an evil or something else we don't take time to understand. My uncle also wore a look of sadness and seemed uncomfortable. I figured it was from being in a room full of women. I know when I was a kid, I didn't like being in a room full of women. But the look was probably caused from having a sick feeling inside; he knew some of the facts at the time that I did not.

When my uncle noticed me standing in the doorway of the living room, the expression on his face dropped even lower. He looked down for a moment and then back up as he slowly walked toward me. He put an arm around my shoulders and guided me toward the back of the house and out into the backyard. We stood in the yard facing the trail. We were alone then. It was a sharp contrast from the previous day when there were people milling back and forth in the yard and entering and exiting the trail. The silence was overwhelming, and I was about to ask my uncle what was wrong (though deep down I knew the answer) when he spoke.

"I'm sorry to have to tell you this, George, but we found your sister this morning. There was an accident in the woods, and Katie is no longer with us."

"You mean she's dead!" This wasn't a question on my part. I knew the answer; I just needed to hear it in words of finality.

"Yes, she's dead."

We stood there, silent, for another minute, and then I ran and climbed up into the tree house Tommy and I had built. I hunched into a corner behind a large board so that Uncle Ken couldn't see me, hot tears now wetting my cheeks. There was a small crack at the edge of the board, and, after a minute, I looked through it to where he had been standing. He remained there, looking up unhappily at the tree house. It seemed like a very long time before he turned and went back into the house.

Everything changed for me from that moment on. It didn't matter that it was many years before I knew the whole truth surrounding the circumstances of Katie's death. Even so, her death scarred me deeply. I became very introverted. I played with Tommy less often, and I really didn't want to explore along the trails. My crush on Sherry was itself crushed. I didn't blame anyone—not Tommy, who helped me make the paths where Katie had her accident, or Sherry, whose jutting tooth had mesmerized me so much on that fateful day. I didn't blame them, but the reminders were there nonetheless.

My parents never talked to me in depth about the accident. Of course they were there with me and listened intently when the sheriff questioned me about Katie's disappearance. There wasn't much I could tell him. I didn't see anyone else in the woods; I didn't hear any strange noises. As much as my mother had admonished me about keeping an eye on Katie along the trails, she never said anything after the incident. Both she and my father must have known how I felt. And as parents they were facing their own grief and pain.

Though my relationship with my friends deteriorated greatly after the accident, it didn't really matter that much because our family moved before winter set in. But even by then, I had started to hear rumors that Katie's death was more than just an accident. At the time, they were rumors and whispers between others that I caught just whiffs of. And as I had my own demons to confront and really didn't want to talk about Katie with others I didn't pursue the matter with them.

But the whispers stayed in my mind. Years later, when I started to see a therapist, he said that most assuredly the remnants of that incident from my childhood played a major role in me becoming a writer and the topics I chose to write about. But for my own edification—maybe my own sanity—I had to learn if the whispers and rumors were true. I've heard people say it might be better sometimes if you don't try to find the truth. In some cases it might be true, but in this instance, finding the truth was something I had to do. The nightmares had already started. A part of both my conscious and subconscious mind already knew the truth, so I guess the journey I needed to take was not to learn the truth but to face it. Even though I was certain what the truth was, I needed to see it in writing, read it, and discover the details.

Probably the first thing I learned, even before I began digging into the facts, was why my mother had thought something was wrong that evening so long ago. And it was more of a feeling than a thought. When

I had children of my own, I knew. It's some kind of instinctual bond. Unfortunately not all parents have it, but then not everyone should be a parent. Most of us have a connection with our children and can sense when something is not right.

I decided to start my quest before my parents passed on, but I still couldn't bring myself to ask them about Katie. Our relationship had returned to some semblance of normalcy, but their eyes always seemed a little dim and their voices a little hollow. I had asked my wife one time if she noticed it, and she said no, but then she hadn't gone through what my parents and I had. And she hadn't known them before the incident. My parents' lives perked up a little when we gave them a granddaughter. That's not to say they weren't happy when my wife and I had a baby boy first. I couldn't ask any more of them as grandparents. It's just that Loralei was a girl, and I believed it helped to mend some of the pain they felt over Katie. They doted on her and really seemed to enjoy it when they had a chance to babysit. Before they were killed by a drunk driver—another form of monster we live with in this world—my daughter had developed many features that reminded me of Katie. I could see in my parents' eyes that they also saw the resemblance, and it seemed to strengthen their bond with her.

When my parents died, my wife and I became even more dependent on her parents to watch Loralei when Margo and I had plans. I had never felt comfortable with just an average babysitter watching over Loralei; it had to be either Margo's parents or mine. And most of the time, it had been my parents. It wasn't that I didn't trust my in-laws, but I knew my parents felt the same caution I did. Margo had even explained to her parents (or as much as she knew) why I was so protective of Loralei.

This feeling of wanting to know the truth and to unburden myself was even more compelling after my parents died because then I had to put more trust in my in-laws. And to find the truth was not that hard; it had always been there waiting for me. Often the truth, mired and obscured in facts of reality, is just waiting to be discovered or, in my case, to be faced and understood. In the broadest sense of the word Katie was involved in an accident that day. But it was not an accident in the way my parents and the other adults wanted me to believe when I was a boy. Instead, it was an evil, planned, and man-made accident that befell Katie. It was the truth of that accident I went in search of.

The town I grew up in as a child—the town that had gone from sunshine and laughs and a pretty jutting tooth to a place of darkness and fear—had not grown much in population over the years. The police had advanced as much into the computer age as they needed to, but the records concerning Katie's death were still on paper files in folders in the basement of the station. Either they didn't have the money or the desire to pay someone to input the old information into the computers. But the information was still there; the truth was waiting for me.

I called the police before journeying home, so the information I wanted had been retrieved before I arrived. When I gave them my request, I wondered if they were only too willing to help because they knew who I was. Did they think they could find something about my past that wasn't publicly known? People love to uncover information about the famous. Truthfully, though, I didn't care.

One of the officers, a middle-aged woman who appeared to be uncomfortable around me, led me to a room where I could be by myself. Her attitude confirmed to me that she was privy to what was in the files. She gave me a weak smile as she closed the door behind her, encasing me in the room with my past. When I turned to look at the table in the room, I was inclined to think it was an interrogation room. I was taken aback by how slender the folder was that lay on the table. I eyed it suspiciously as I sat down in one of the two chairs in the room.

For the heavy burden I had carried with me over the years as a result of the incident, the folder seemed to hold so little. For a few minutes I silently looked at the folder, not quite ready to open it. I could feel the tension racing through me, a tension that had steadily built from the time I decided on this course of action. It is easy to make a choice to do something but harder to put that choice into action. Sometimes we fear what we know we'll learn, and I was pretty sure what the facts were that lay before me.

I slowly reached out and grabbed the corner of the folder, hesitating one last moment before opening it. It was a multiple pocket folder with five different sections, each pocket containing a separate aspect of the incident and its investigation. Before I pulled the papers from each pocket, I read the description on the little tabs and analyzed some of the contents I needed to see and some I didn't. Eventually I ended up with four piles of papers on the table; one pocket I left the contents in because I didn't want to see them. As I pulled the papers from the first pocket, what I had suspected over the years was confirmed: Katie's death was more than just an accident; it was a crime.

The first pocket held forms with information on them. The forms themselves were frightening in the fact that we, as a society, were bureaucratically prepared for the evils some of us perpetrate. A chill ran through my heart as I read through the details. This pile of papers only revealed the facts. From an outsider's point of view, this was probably the best way to present the case, but because I was intimate with what had happened, I felt the lack of compassion on the pages. It was so cold and impersonal. The sadness I felt over this quickly changed as the information grew more complex.

I understand now the burden my parents carried after that day and why their demeanors changed so much. It was more than just having a child die; that in itself is enough to dramatically alter someone for life.

But in this case it was how she died. Tears rolled hotly over my cheeks as I read the words on the pages. I was hot from pain, hot from grief, hot from anger. Katie had been brutalized in so many ways. Not only was she murdered but she was sexually abused beforehand. It made me sick to think of the ordeal she had gone through.

So while she had been alive, Katie had been raped. If that wasn't enough, when the monster was done with her, he had tortured her for a while before she died. I've written horrible stories of what monsters and creatures have done to humans. I've seen many horror movies whose directors' main purpose is to see who can make the bloodiest, goriest, and most realistic death scenes. Some people can't stand that kind of hardcore horror, but it has never turned me off. But reading about what happened to my little sister sickened me. I had guessed, but reading the details was so much different than what I had imagined. It was like knowing the truth but not having to accept it until you read the facts. Now I could no longer hope that Katie's death was an accident.

The second folder held typed-up pages of interviews with individuals involved. Most of the interviews were with people I would, in a sense, call victims also, namely, my parents and me. There were some statements by others who had given what they thought were clues: a car seen driving in the vicinity or a stranger hanging around the area and the like. But the bulk of the pages were the statements from the immediate family. I was really interested in the statements my parents had given, for though I never got the impression in words or looks that they blamed me for what had happened, maybe they had said something different to the investigators.

I read through each of my parents statements three times. There was no indication from either of them that they blamed me for Katie's death. I was glad for that but not for my benefit. I will probably carry my own guilt until the day I die. I had accepted that fact—not that the acceptance made my life any easier. The nightmares still haunted my sleeping hours, and Katie's screams for me still echoed in my mind. For years I believed it was just a terrible accident. Even with the whispered rumors I had heard soon after her death, it wasn't until I had matured more that I could make a logical supposition of what had happened. My relief was for my parents. It's hard to imagine the grief they must have felt each day over the loss of Katie and to know from the start all the circumstances surrounding her death. It would have been even more unbearable for them if they had blamed me.

My own statements shed no new light on what I remembered from that day. There was no piece of the puzzle I had locked away in my subconscious mind waiting to be retrieved. I had not reported seeing or hearing anything I had since forgotten about. In the written words of what I had spoken I could hear the innocence of childhood. It came through in powerful tones. We all gradually lose that innocence as we mature. Some of us start to lose it earlier than others; I can point to that summer when mine really began to leave me, eroding away in chunks. When the innocence departs in ways that are not normal, it leaves open sores on the soul that may never heal.

The third pocket was the one I had decided not to look at, so its contents were still there. It was filled with photos from the crime scene. And these I definitely didn't want to see, especially after everything I had suspected over the years. A trick that successful writers and filmmakers use in their craft is knowing just how much to tell or show their audience. If they take people to just a certain point and then stop, the reader's or viewer's imagination fills in the rest of the story. People can imagine such horrible things.

Maybe if I looked at the photos, it might lessen the images my mind created when I read about the incident. Yes, the words had sharply pierced into my heart, and the images that formed in my mind were added to the horrors that will haunt me for the rest of my life. What I wouldn't give to change the images that those words had created in my mind, but I still couldn't bring myself to look at the photos. It was my sister, after all, so young and innocent—the one I had failed. Would her lifeless eyes be open, staring accusingly at me? Would her mouth still be shaped to the screams of pain she must have uttered as she died, or would it look as though she had been calling to me, as she did in my nightmares? I could not face those possibilities.

The fourth pocket held papers and pictures of people who must have been suspects and who had been interviewed. After looking at the first picture of a suspect, I realized there was no need to look through all the papers from that pocket. It only took a second of looking at the picture to determine in my mind that the person was guilty. Instantly I was filled with anger and hatred toward an individual who could well be innocent. I'm sure I would feel the same way toward any suspect I saw a picture of, so there was no need to continue. Nothing could be gained by it.

What I was surprised to find out about myself was the depth of hatred I had been harboring over the years. My own perceived guilt had been a constant companion from the time of Katie's death. It was there even before I began to figure out the truth, cradled in the knowledge that she died when she was supposed to be in my care. The hatred must have crept in with the whispers and rumors. It shadowed me on the outskirts of my guilt, lurking in silence even as it grew in intensity.

Reading what had happened to Katie and seeing just one picture of someone who had been suspected of the crime brought the hate and anger to the forefront. I was scared by the ferociousness of the hatred and the immediate thoughts about ways to make the monster responsible for Katie's death pay with so much pain. It was clear in my mind what I would do, the viciousness with which I would attack the perpetrator. My mind was working like it did when I was in the middle of writing one of my stories. Everything in the real world around me was blocked out.

Unlike the state I experienced while writing one of my stories, in this one I was not a participant but an observer watching myself. In my writing visions, for lack of a better description, I had control over myself or the character I was portraying and could direct the outcome any way I wanted. If need be, I could even rewind it and have a do-over. In this vision I was just an observer, and I could not believe the evil I saw in my eyes, the sadistic grin spread across my lips every time the human monster screamed out in pain. And because I had seen a picture of one of the people of interest at the time, the monster now had a face. If I looked at more of the pictures, I could imagine torturing the monster over and over again, each time with the monster having a different appearance. They couldn't all be guilty, at least not of the crime against Katie. And I didn't want to keep living that hatred.

The final pocket held papers giving an overview of the crime and a wrap-up of the investigation. There wasn't much to learn in the pages except for one major truth: the crime was unsolved. Unfortunately, that was also how I still felt—unresolved. I had hoped this journey might bring closure to the pain and guilt that molded me into the person I had become. Even though many would consider my life successful—in many respects it was—I would give up the fame and fortune to be free of the nightmares that awaken me most nights, the voices and screams for help that haunt even my waking hours.

So as I head back home from my little journey, I am prepared to fully answer my son's question. It is time to tell him for the sake of his little sister. No, there are no monsters under his bed—not like the ones his father writes about. But yes, there are monsters in the world, and they are so much worse than anything his father has described because those monsters are real.

Printed in the United States
By Bookmasters